A Thousand Threads: Stories of Us is a collaborative writing initiative for trans and gender-diverse people, co-produced by Alex Nichols and Urszula Dawkins. Contact us at athousandthreads@lightblue.com.au

ISBN: 978-0-6454294-0-4

Editors: Alex Nichols and Urszula Dawkins, with author-editors Charlie, D, Driplets, Jocelyn, Sam and Sarah

Cover artwork and section headings: Onezee State
Book design: Urszula Dawkins and Alex Nichols

This project has been supported by:

We Twinkle Like Gold was produced at River Studios, West Melbourne.

We Twinkle Like Gold

A Thousand Threads: Stories of Us, Volume I

Writing and artwork by trans and gender-diverse creatives
from Naarm and beyond, 2021–22

THOUSAND THREADS PRESS
MELBOURNE

Acknowledgement of country

We gratefully acknowledge the Wurundjeri and Boonwurrung, Wathaurong, Dja Dja Wurrung, Kaurna, Gadigal, Dharug, Yuin and Waka Waka peoples as the traditional custodians of various lands on which *We Twinkle Like Gold* was created. We pay our respects to Elders past and present and emerging leaders and extend our respects to all First Nations people across this continent.

Australia is not a new country. Its history dates back over 60,000 years, as home to the oldest living, surviving culture anywhere on Earth. We thank the traditional custodians across this continent for their continued care for country.

We live, work and play on land that was forcibly taken from Aboriginal and Torres Strait Islander people. We recognise these past atrocities and that Australia was founded on genocide and dispossession of First Nations people. We acknowledge the harm caused by systems and institutions that were built and continue to be structured to exclude and oppress First Nations people.

We acknowledge that Paying the Rent honours the sovereignty of Aboriginal people. But whilst this may be a more just way of living on this stolen land, as non-Indigenous people we must also advocate for and show solidarity with those whose country we now live on, to promote, defend and support land justice and the continued fight for Treaty.

Sovereignty has never been ceded. It always was and always will be Aboriginal land.

Sam

There are many other stolen lands across this Earth, and we acknowledge the First Peoples of each and every one of them.

From D:
To the Abuela I never met and to the veins that link us to land we call Ayacucho in Peru at this point in time. Thanks for keeping the flame. Oh you are Glorious!
To the Abuelo that took her from us, you had the guts but forgot the heart.
To the world-wide community, what were you thinking?
To Dios, we are still waiting.

Contents

Images

Page **23,** Ze; page **37**, T.; pages **42** and **43**, D, with T.; page **45**, D, cluster exercise; pages **52** to **57**, Ze, *Tightrope*; page **68**, Juho Luomala; pages **102** and **103**, Ze, *The Ongoing River Self*; page **105**, D; page **153**, D; page **159**, Ze

Foreword, 2022:
What the workshop meant to me

I don't really know what prompted me to sign up for this workshop. All I knew was that I needed to write. Not that I had any reason to believe I could create anything worthwhile out of it. I wasn't an avid reader, let alone writer.

So it was a surprise to me to discover that I could actually write. On the whole, I found that sharing space with other queer people helped fill a cup that I didn't know I had. I found writing to be cathartic, and putting things down on (virtual) paper helped me make sense of my lived experiences.

In a world that is so determined to misunderstand us, it's been healing and hopeful to see all of us as our diverse selves, telling our stories. Over the course of our collaboration, I learned not just that I can write, but also that I don't have to write sad stories. We can write funny stories, thought-provoking pieces and also fantastical fantasies that centre us in our storytelling.

The world is struggling with a reckoning that the privileged have gotten away with for centuries. Unseen voices are now being heard. We are gaining visibility; our rights are starting to gain recognition. We are starting to learn to be proud of who we are. But as recent events show, they can be taken away in an instant. Our pride is temporal, our freedoms can be fleeting and our rights are fragile.

We have come a long way from Marsha and Sylvia to Sarah and Danica, and Asia Kate, MJ and Elliot. Yet the stories out there are not ours. Much of the narrative out there is about how the cis see us—body parts, intimate violence, whether they are comfortable with us in their spaces. Our lived experiences are more varied, simple and complex than that. The experience of falling in love with your body, which is neither sexual nor narcissistic. The struggle to exist in the world that continually erases our identities. The joy of simply being queer…of simply being.

This collection offers the reader an opportunity to walk in our shoes, if they so choose, and maybe, if they are open, to be led to an understanding of the diversity of the human experience and different ways to be.

You're welcome.

Sarah

Foreword, 2047:
How far we've come

We live in a time where the Gender Wars have been and gone, and we're pretty lucky to be free of the constraints of specific gender roles and arbitrary divisions of society along the lines of which set of genitals we were born with. Those were times of great pain for trans and gender-diverse people.

I, myself, came of age during that time. I remember the great sadness and distress I felt back then, every time I read a new article about the harassment or murder of trans and gender-diverse people who weren't lucky enough to live in one of the more tolerant countries or states.

All of us can link our own stories back to those who have come before us and see these links like a thousand threads, just as the name suggests. I really felt like I could see myself in a lot of the pieces. Some of them even had my name, which was kind of eerie at first.

The first time I read this volume, I felt all sorts of complex emotions. The confusion and raw emotion expressed in some of these pieces brought back my own gender journey, which, in my time, was also one of transition. Even writing this now, I feel myself getting a bit choked up as I re-experience the fear in some of these pieces.

When I look through these pieces I somehow feel extraordinarily proud to be among the last people to identify themselves as trans, and I am immensely grateful to be living in a time where these struggles are no longer necessary for people to just be who they are.

As we look to our future with hope, free of binary gender constraints, expectations or labels like cis and trans, I think it's helpful to look back on where we've come from and to remember the pain and isolation people felt only a few decades ago so that we appreciate the freedoms we have now. People who were guilty of nothing more than trying to live as their authentic selves struggled and died in great enough numbers that the rest of society started to take notice and examine their own roles in allowing it to happen before they decided enough was enough. Despite militant opposition, these people twinkled like gold in some very difficult circumstances, finding euphoria, meaning and a sense of self wherever they could.

So it is with great pleasure that I recommend this volume to you, however you identify in your own gender expression journey. I hope that it helps you understand where we've all come from and encourages you too to twinkle like gold.

Take these pages from the past and celebrate how far we've come as communities in celebrating everyone in their diversity now, no matter how it manifests.

Debbie

Before we begin, a content warning

We Twinkle Like Gold includes material that is playful, experimental, heartfelt, serious and exploratory, written by a group of people whose life experiences are all very different. Some of the stories may be hard for some people to read, and what's empowering for one reader may bring up painful memories for another. As such, we haven't tried to guess how each piece may impact. Please take care as you read, and know that whatever brings you to these pages, we wish you well.

If something comes up that feels overwhelming, reach out for support. A couple of helplines for queer, trans and gender-diverse folk are:

Rainbow Door (Victoria)
rainbowdoor.org.au
Call: 1800 729 367
SMS: 0480 017 246
Email: support@rainbowdoor.org.au

QLife (Australia-wide)
qlife.org.au
Call: 1800 184 527 or webchat

"My right to be me is tied with a thousand threads
to your right to be you."

Leslie Feinberg

The Little Changeling: The Wrong Child

Why should the changeling be upset? It has everything it wants, hiding away out of sight. It doesn't know how lucky it is to have the choice to stay out of the world, to be able to simply decide not to engage. What a lucky little creature it is, to have us standing between it and the world it so desperately wants to avoid. What a pitiful little creature, to have the entire world at its fingertips but not take it, to hide instead in fantasy and fascination. Of course we will be here waiting for it, for what choice do we have when all the power it musters is to cling so strongly to where it is comfortable?

Should we force it out? Should we leave it be? Are those our only options? Why won't it talk to us? Why won't it let us help it? Why does it stay in there, day in and day out? Is it happy? Sad? Does it need? Does it want? Does it know who we are? Does it know who it is? Does it want us here? Does it want us in there?

It's led us before into its worlds, but it's so hard to follow, so hard to understand even when it tries, and it so very rarely tries. How does it know all about these far-away worlds yet barely understands where we are? Where does it go when it closes that door? What is contained in the light and sound it pumps into its eyes and ears, day in and day out? Is it learning anything new? Does it revise the old? Does it know about us? Does it know about anyone? What is it doing?

Surely we could teach it. Surely we should teach it. Surely we're able to teach it. We know how to teach the real children; surely a pretender will be little different. Surely it will want to learn alongside them, do the things they do for fear of… Well, what would it fear? We will treat it as we treat the real children.

Its behaviour unsettles us. It has not harmed us—would not, in fact. It is too polite. It follows the rules set down for it but does not seem to realise why. It attempts to speak to the real children but does not seem to understand how. It does whatever we ask of it but does not seem to care for the outcome of its work. In fact, it does not seem to care about anything. How do you teach something that is only ever politely waiting to get away from you?

We wonder if it knows. Whether it sees the others and realises they are kin, or somehow thinks it actually belongs with the real children. Perhaps neither—it only tries to talk to one or the other when it has to, or maybe when the loneliness becomes too great. Does it see anything in the world like itself? Perhaps that's why it carries those books around —it has exhausted its search here, it must cast its net further afield, to other worlds. Such a shame to lose a creature with so much potential in the pages of fiction. Oh well, what is there to be done? At least it does not disrupt the real children too much. That would be the true travesty.

It spends far too much time exploring these other worlds. We need it to stay here, to learn what to do in this one, but it will not stay put. It is clever, and it gets by, but that will not always be enough, and it should know that. What does it expect to do outside of our protection? It fantasises about inviting the real people into its worlds, getting by in this world as a tour guide for others. Of course, what else even could it do? Does it realise the fuss it causes through its failures? Does it realise the sideshow it is, trying to whore out its meaningless explorations for our entertainment, while the real people work and study? It won't get far.

Where is the real child whose place it took, we wonder? Perhaps he is trapped in one of these fantasy worlds, struggling to fit in with the changeling's kin as we so struggle with it. Or perhaps he is celebrated —a real person must be a rarity among all those impostors. Or perhaps the most frightening possibility is that he is both. That poor child, what do they want from him? What do they expect of him? Is he there for a reason? If only there were some way to help him. He must feel so scared, so alone in that place not meant for him. If only he could know that somewhere out there, there are people like him, people who would understand him, people who he might know how to talk to. If only we had him here.

Driplets

Anna & Dion

Anna: Is magic really real?

Dion: I think I've seen something magical before. That makes me think it's real. What do you think?

Anna: Really? What was it? Please tell me??

Dion: I think I saw a ghost…

Anna: Was it a scary ghost?

Dion: No, it was a cheeky ghost. I was at my mum's house, and I kept trying to turn off this show, *Wheel of Fortune*, and every time I turned it off, it would magically turn back on!?!

Anna: That's definitely a ghost!! I wish I could see ghosts. And fairy godmothers, like in the stories!

Dion: I know, right!?! And also mermaids. Mermaids are definitely real. I actually think I might be a real-life mermaid.

Anna: I WISH I was a mermaid.

Dion: If you could have ANY superpower, what would it be?

Anna: Definitely to be able to swim like a dolphin. That would be amazing. Swimming all day and playing with the dolphins. They look like they are so happy and having so much fun!

Dion: So cool! I think my superpower would be…flying. Sometimes I feel a bit stuck, and I think flying would make me feel really free.

Anna: You could be a flying mermaid! You would be stunning!

Dion: Okay, so a little secret. I'm actually a water polo champion and I LOVEEE clothes, like I love creating an outfit that is…like almost a picture using colours and glitter and prints. I stand out and sometimes people stare. But my superpower is…not caring, because I get to be me and that's the mo—

Anna: I wish I could have that superpower. I'm not allowed to wear the clothes I want to…

Dion: If you could wear anything, what would it be?

Kate & Ripley

DISCORD.

HOPE + POSSIBILITY

INVITING + CONNECT

FIND COMFORT IN UNCOMFORTABLE SITUATION

PART OF IT

OTHERWORLDLY

LIMITLESSNESS

The Little Changeling: Acting Normally

"I wish you could just act normally—then it might be safer for you."

She had a point. Perhaps if it could have done a better job at learning to act like the real children, think like the real children, be like the real children, it wouldn't have so much to worry about. Then it could focus on the important things in life.

And yet, for the first time, the little changeling was starting to recognise that it simply was not like the real children. No longer in the reactive way of rejecting what had rejected it, but accepting that it could not find its blueprint for the self where it had grown up. Nor could it find that blueprint anywhere in the human world. It had no idea where to start, but for once it had a heading towards self-understanding. Would a real human have abandoned something like that to instead remain on an island of safety?

It didn't blame them. Being hated was hard, but for once it was being noticed as well, and that was perhaps worse.

What IS acting normally? I mean, If I could do that, obviously I would! I don't understand why the others seem to hate me. I've tried everything to try and be just like them, but it's always not quite right and I don't get what I'm doing wrong… They all seem to be able to do and say and think the right things in the right way all the time, and everyone just accepts it. How come they don't accept that from me? Why can't I just think the same way they all think?

Maybe if I can figure out what I am, then I can start to act and think in that way, and once I make sense, the others will stop hating me. But will they stop noticing how different I am? I'm actually starting to feel scared! And I don't get why. I mean, the human children think differently to me, but that doesn't make me scared of them. It doesn't make me hate them. Why should they hate me for being different?

It's not fair! I don't want to be different, but I can't help it. I just am! I wish they could understand that and just let me be me. It makes me feel so sad sometimes, and that's bad enough—but now she's telling me I should be scared as well? Why is normal so safe when it's so boring and alien at times? I don't want to learn to act and think like the real children, but I kind of have to if I'm going to be safe...

The little changeling sighed and quietly followed mother down the street.

Driplets

My Name Is Debbie

The not-yet-girl lay in bed, turning over the events of that afternoon in their head. They'd just been spinning on the monkey bars and talking with the girls when they'd left to visit the toilets. On the way, they'd walked past the boys, and one of them, Tommy, had called out to them and asked:

"Why are you always hanging around with the girls instead of playing footy with us?"

They'd answered, "Coz I don't like footy?", not sure where that answer was going to get them.

Tommy had then said, "How can you not like footy? You're a boy. If you like hanging around with the girls so much, you should be one. I'm gonna call you Debbie since you like being a girl so much! Bye, Debbie!"

Tommy had laughed as he'd jogged back into the game. The not-yet-girl had glanced back as they walked on towards the toilet block and saw a group of the boys looking their way and laughing. On the way back to the monkey bars, the not-yet-girl had again glanced over at the boys playing footy and being aggressive with each other. This was one of the reasons why they didn't play. The aggression made no sense and it scared them. There were other reasons of course. The rules were impossible to follow, the positions on the field sounded ridiculous and made no sense, and of course, bouncing an egg-shaped ball required coordination skills that the not-yet-girl simply didn't have.

They remembered sighing, shaking their head and going back to their friends, who were styling each other's hair with hair ties. They remembered the pull in their gut as they watched the girls gathering up each other's long hair—wishing that their own hair was long enough to be tied back like the girls could do. Their own hair was longer than most of the boys', except for Adam's, but it wasn't long enough to make a ponytail like so many of the girls had.

They remembered becoming aware of some raised voices and looking over at the boys' group, noticing that some of them were laughing and one of them was yelling. The one yelling had been Adam, their best friend. As Adam stalked away from the group of laughing boys, one of them seemed to throw an insult at him which made some of the other boys laugh. Adam had shaken his head and ignored it, and the game had continued on—but not before he had looked over at the not-yet-girl with a frown on his face.

They turned all these events over and over in their mind.

"If you like hanging around with the girls so much, you should be one"…

It was obviously supposed to be an insult, but was it really? There didn't seem to be anything wrong with being a girl. Girls weren't expected to play sports. Girls could spend as much time in the library as they liked. Girls talked to each other about all sorts of things and supported each other. Girls were *nice* to each other.

Boys seemed to have all these rules. They were supposed to like sport and they had to be good at it, or else they'd be told, 'You run (or throw or bat or whatever) like a girl' as if that was a bad thing. Boys weren't supposed to spend any more time in the library than they were forced to. Boys were supposed to be aggro and rough and always try to be better than someone else. Boys were supposed to be 'tough'. They were supposed to swear and spit, and they weren't supposed to cry when they got hurt.

Being a girl seemed way more sensible than being a boy. If they were a girl, then the not-yet-girl wouldn't have to have a 'girlfriend' all the time just to have an excuse to spend more time with their friends who were girls. Of course then their friendship with Adam might look a bit weird. But it would be worth it to have long hair and be able to do all the things the girls could do.

And maybe Debbie wasn't such a bad name. Their mother had let them wear a dress once, during the summer holidays. They'd felt so free and happy, dancing around in the sun, dodging under the water sprinkler with their sister. Their mother had called them 'Davina' while they were in the dress. It had sounded like such a silly, old-fashioned name, as much dress-up as the dress itself. They'd had to change back into their 'normal' clothes before their father came home, which had been disappointing. But it had only been a game...

Debbie was a much more suitable name than Davina. The not-yet-girl imagined themselves with long hair tied back into a ponytail with a coloured hair tie, and their friends calling out 'Hi Debbie!' when they arrived at school. It didn't seem so bad. In fact, it sounded pretty good! As they drifted off to sleep, their last thought was, 'I wish I really was a girl'.

<>

The next morning as they walked through the school gate, they heard a chorus of 'Hi Debbie!', but it wasn't from their friends. It was from that group of boys that were laughing the day before, and they were laughing again.

As they put their head down and tried to ignore the mocking, the not-yet-girl thought to themselves that boys were awful—and they didn't want to be one if they had to be like that. They kept to themselves for the next several minutes, until it was time to go into the classroom, but their thoughts kept turning around all morning. Thoughts like, 'I wish I wasn't a boy' and 'I wish I could be a girl' and 'I could never be pretty like Joanne' and 'I could be broad and strong and still be a girl like Fiona is, maybe…'

Several times after thinking things like these, they'd look up and see their smart friend, Tamara, watching them and looking worried.

When they left the classroom for lunch, Tamara walked down the stairs with them. As they started off towards the monkey bars at the other end of the building, Tamara grabbed their arm and dragged them around the other side of the building, to the grassed area that was usually off limits to students during recess and lunchtime. They wondered what was going on—why Tamara was pushing them around and why she looked kind of worried. When they tried to move away, Tamara grabbed their arm again, steered them towards the middle of the grass between two nice-looking garden beds, pushed them down and sat down next to them, still holding onto their arm.

"What's going on?" they both asked at once. The not-yet-girl looked at their friend with wide, questioning eyes.

Tamara took a deep breath and said, "I saw what happened with the boys yesterday, and I heard them this morning. I get why you'd be upset and sad today, but you've been something else. You've been quiet, yeah, but you keep touching your hair and smiling, and talking to yourself… I know something's up, but you don't look like you today. Tell me—what's going on? I want to help. I don't think you're okay, and I'm worried."

They looked up at their friend's sincere face, squeezed back at the hand that was holding theirs, and sighed. "Tommy told me that since I like hanging around with girls so much, I should just be one, and he started calling me Debbie. I hated it and wanted it to stop, but then I was thinking about it last night and—" They stopped talking as tears started to well in their eyes.

"What is it, D?", their friend asked gently, still squeezing their hand and rubbing their arm with the other.

The not-yet-girl took a couple of wobbly breaths and whispered. "It sounds stupid, but I really wish I *was* a girl. I mean, I kind of feel like I *am* a girl, inside, but for some reason I look like a boy, outside and… I… hate… it…", they gasped out, in between sobs.

Tamara threw her arms around her friend and hugged them tightly to her, rubbing their back, letting them cry quietly into her shoulder.

As they rocked back and forth, Tamara said quietly, "You know, I've always pretty much thought of you as a girl with short hair and a boy's name who just doesn't like wearing dresses. I'd definitely still be your friend if you were a girl. You're too smart to be a boy really, anyway!" They both laughed then, and Tamara pulled away to look at her friend's face. They gave a small smile.

"Okay", Tamara said, with gentle determination. "What do you want to do?"

"About what?" they asked, feeling confused.

"About being a girl, D. Obviously!" Tamara responded as only she could. She was always so confident and certain when she had an answer for something.

"But I can't be a girl! Look at me. Everybody knows I'm a boy. They're already teasing and calling me Debbie. And anyway, I can't suddenly just change into a girl. What would my mum say?"

"Oh, I think your mum would probably surprise you. And I hate to break it to you, but I think you're wrong. I think you *can* be a girl if you want to. You have the spirit of a girl. You know, that attitude and the—". She frowned in thought for a moment before brightening up and declaring,

"—and the essence! That's the word I was after. You have the *essence* of a girl!"

Tamara stood up, hauling the not-yet-girl up to their feet, and walked around them, looking them over and frowning in concentration while the not-yet-girl stood there, waiting for Tamara to finish thinking.

"Okay", Tamara finally said, "Let's go and hang around with the others, and then after school, you go home and think about who you would be as a girl—what you like to wear, what your name would be, what you'd be interested in and how you'd want to act. I'm going to do my own research, and we'll reconvene tomorrow to strategise. *That* means we'll meet up again tomorrow and make some plans, so you'd better make some notes as you go", they said in their know-it-all tone, which made the not-yet-girl roll their eyes and smile.

Tamara had a project—and she always worked really hard on her projects, and they were beautiful. And with that thought worming its way into their brain, the not-yet-girl followed their friend around the back of the building and towards the monkey bars, and they competed with the other girls and each other to see how many spins they could each do before they got dizzy enough to fall over.

‹◊›

That evening, the not-yet-girl didn't watch TV. They did their homework and then sat in their room with their notebook and thought about everything Tamara had said at lunchtime. They started writing things in their notebook. If they were a girl, what would they like to wear? They would like to wear a dress. Something with a gathered skirt that could flare out when they spun around, but would still hang about to their knees, giving them lots of movement. Oh, and they'd be able to wear some nice sandals or those girls' school shoes—what were they called, Mary Janes?—instead of the clunky, heavy boys' shoes they were forced to wear all the time. And maybe sometimes they'd wear jeans but with a V-neck top with flowers or something colourful and pretty on it, or maybe even a nice, puffy blouse with one of those rounded collars. But most of all, they'd want their ears pierced, so they could wear a flash of colour there like most of their friends did.

Next on the list was their name. That was confusing, because Debbie was actually a pretty good name but the boys were using it to make fun of them, so it might not work. Tamara called them 'D' when it was just the two of them, and they called her 'T', so that could work. But up until now it had just been their special way of sharing something together. But it wouldn't be strange to hear, so it was worth putting on the list. Their sister had confided once that she wished she could change her name to Allison. That was a nice name, but their sister wouldn't like them stealing it, and they needed to have her on their side in case Mum didn't like the idea of them being a girl…

As for what they'd be interested in or how they would act, none of that really had to change, did it? They liked reading, they liked listening to music, they liked singing and learning the piano. The only sports they didn't completely suck at were rounders and netball, which were girls' sports, so maybe they could do one or both of those? And how would they act? Surely that would be just the same? They wouldn't have to pretend to have any interest in sport or cars. They could still ride a bike, but maybe they could get something different than their BMX. Oh—but most importantly, they would grow their hair and tie it back in a ponytail!

As they drifted off to sleep this night, they idly wondered what Tamara would be doing her research on. If they were her project and all her projects came out looking beautiful, maybe they could look beautiful… They fell asleep with that thought in their head and a smile on their face.

<o>

The next morning the not-yet-girl walked around the block and went into the school through a different gate. They'd woken up feeling nervous but positive about today's 'strategising session' with Tamara and didn't want a bunch of rude, idiot boys spoiling their good mood. They caught up with their friend Amanda from the other class by walking in that way, and they realised that Amanda was another person who treated them just like one of the girls. They pondered this until they found themselves being ushered into the library with the rest of their class. They heard a sharp hiss behind them and off to the left, and saw Tamara with a pile of notes and printouts, sitting at one of the study carrels in a corner where nobody ever went.

As soon as they'd sat down, Tamara held out her hand for their notes. They handed them over and waited while their friend read through them, smiling.

"Why are you smiling—did I write something funny?", they asked nervously.

"No, of course not. You wrote pretty much what I thought you'd write, and I think Operation Gender Reveal is going to be a success", she said smugly.

"Operation Gender Reveal???!!!", they hissed, eyes wide with panic.

"Relax, D. I really think this is going to work out much better than you could probably imagine right now, and I'm pretty excited for you", she said warmly as she reached out to rest a hand reassuringly on their arm.

"I'm pretty sure you're what's called 'transgender', and if you are, there are rules about how the school has to treat you and look after you, because it's against the law to bully people for being gender diverse now. So they'll have to stop the teasing. And they'll have to let you wear a dress if you want to.

"And here's the best part—are you ready?", she asked, looking expectantly at her friend.

The not-yet-girl nodded slowly, already starting to feel overwhelmed with where this conversation seemed to be going.

"The best part," Tamara said, as she reached her other hand over to squeeze theirs, "is that I'm pretty sure your mum will be on your side, because *she's* the one who wrote this policy." She glanced down at one of the sheets of printed policy in her lap, shaking her head in wonder as she said, "In fact, I wouldn't be surprised if your mum saw this coming and developed this policy specifically to make sure you'd be able to do what we're talking about".

"But what *are* we talking about here?", asked the not-yet-girl, with a mix of excitement and fear.

"We're talking about you coming out as transgender and being a girl— for real", she replied.

They could see the excitement shining in her eyes and the genuine warmth in her gaze, and their own eyes started to water as an unfamiliar feeling started burning in their gut and rising up into their chest. As they felt the shape of their face changing and the feeling spreading through their whole body, they realised that this feeling was hope—and that they were smiling broadly, genuinely, in a way they hadn't smiled in a long time, as the thought hit home that they could actually, really, truly be themselves.

They wiped the tears of happiness from their eyes and looked at their friend, who asked, "First things first—what do *you* think we should do first, D?"

They took a deep breath, squeezed Tamara's hands in their own, looked her in the eye and said, "First thing? The first thing I'm going to do is tell you that my name is Debbie, and I'm a girl".

Jocelyn, with Driplets

That Ember of Tenderness

It was colder than I'd ever felt before. The memory is foggy, but the air was still and crystal clear, broken by the thrill and excitement that hung in the air along with my frozen clouds of breath. The grass, the street, the roofs of the houses were all dusted with white. I remember a hedge, black against the snow. I could hear the squeaking and rustling of my puffa jacket and felt the wet shock of cold through my corduroy pants as I knelt on the ground. I had no gloves, so my time was limited, but I was determined to see my task through, painstakingly sculpting snow into tiny spheres. It bit at my palms, worse than how the air bit at my cheeks and nose. When my hands were frozen and pink with cold, I had to go back inside to the warmth of the fire, but I remember lovingly staring at my tiny snowman with twigs for a face and arms.

<>

I'm on a beach, the wind whipping my hair into a frenzy, cold against my face. I trudge along the cliffside, following the coastline in the sand, feeling the gritty salt and sand against my skin. The sky is grey and melts into the water, which laps against the dull shore. I am not looking at the sky. I am staring at my feet, looking at one move in front of the other as I walk.

Against the cliffside there is a dark shape. I rush to it, pushing the salt-encrusted hair out of my face to see…a body. It is still, unmoving, only about half my size, and I feel tears spring to my eyes as I see the dirty blue and white feathers, dark beak and cloudy eyes. A fairy penguin, washed up lifeless on the shore. I sob in grief for this bird that I never knew, and I beg my parents to let me bury it. I pile sand on top of its tiny body, and I decorate its grave with shells.

<>

The childhood experiences that stay with me are those of excitement, of tenderness, of deep love of the slightest things. I have tried to keep that ember of tenderness glowing within me, even despite the hardships and cynicism that pervade. I will continue to take wonder in the snow and the stars, to excite in the thrill of a new environment, and to mourn the loss of even the tiniest birds. To be a man with a tender heart is a beautiful thing.

Theo

the lyfe of life is that we if you lie you will die. To die is to live and to live is to die. By Tayika

to love

is die

The Little Changeling: Getting Pixels Stuck in My Toes

I hate the sand. It gets between my toes even when I wear shoes. It sticks to my fingers and then everything I touch, and I can't get rid of it no matter how hard I try. And yet this is where I am, because this is where I should be, because everyone finds this place so relaxing. Searching through each grain, looking for what makes it so, and not an answer to be found. Only the claws and stingers of the creatures who actually belong in this place, and fear stands on respect's pedestal and drives me away from them. There is no reason to be frightened, but I know nothing about this place or these things except the harm they bring even to real people, so what chance do I have? Best to give them a wide berth. Such a shame—such pretty creatures wash up on the shore. What could I have learned if only I'd known how to fear?

Why do we keep coming back here? There's nothing for us but sand and salt and the creatures who don't want us. Is someone forcing us to come here? What contract do we fulfil? What are the consequences if we go too long without grit in our shoes and sun in our eyes? Is it just a practice of the principles you always talk about? We all have to do things we don't want to do. Are you dragging me over the sand and through the water and onto the rocks and up and down and back again to prove it? Or is this one of the things that you *do* want to do, and you simply never thought to ask? Perhaps I tricked you long enough into thinking you made a real person, and this is the sort of thing that real people enjoy. Somehow the perceived kindness would be worse. At least if you knew what you were doing, it would have been intentional.

Don't get the sand in the car. Don't get the sand on the carpet. Be clean before you re-enter. Take nothing of the outside in, bring nothing of the inside out. There is a place for everything; the real world is neat like that. Sand stays outside and does not come with us; books and games stay behind while we come out. The sin occurs when something is outside its place, but what happens when such a place cannot be found? What do we do with the changeling? The pretender? The fake human, the spoiled child? It has no place out here with us, yet the sin also occurs when we see too little of it. If only it could tell us where it belonged.

Such a dramatic little creature. Sneaking around like a baby elephant, adorable how it thinks it's hidden. What reason should it have to desperately try to stay so quiet? There's nothing here that could hurt it. There's nothing here that would hurt it. There's nothing here that should hurt it. The noise is not a crime (except when it is), and the questions we ask when it's out of its place are innocent enough. What are you doing? Why are you doing it? We thought you would be doing something else, but now you are doing this. Has something gone wrong? Have you done something wrong? What is wrong? Where are you going? At least commit your sins where we can see you, you shameful little creature (who we love so much).

The door shut behind me, I return to the comfort of a realm designed for me—by whom, I have a rough idea, but it doesn't matter now. Their creations are now mine to live in, their worlds mine to make sense of. I step out into the sand, revelling in the freedom from the little pieces of the real world that get stuck in my toes, caught in my clothes, crusted into my hair. The little creatures that wash up I can study closely without fear of disturbing them, know their names and what they can do and how they can do them. I can wander along the beach, admire the ocean without being blinded by the glittering sunlight, climb the rocks and explore the rockpools without getting wet or injured.

I dare not look too closely at the letters and pixels that make up the creatures, for fear that measuring the world will cause it to change. I don't climb too far over the rocks. They do not go on forever, and little beyond them was built—the world is over here, not over there. Sometimes I dig my feet a little too far into the sand, hoping to feel all it can give me but finding only the floorboards over which it is spread. I pull my feet back up and keep walking over the surface, not ashamed but feeling for some reason that perhaps I should be.

"What did you do today?" The question I dread. I avoided the world by playing in one designed by someone else. What else would I have done? I certainly have no place in this one—that much has been made exquisitely clear to me each time I've tried to breach it. The things I should know I do not, and each time I do not know I am punished—so what else am I to do but hide from you all? Should I magically have figured it out on my own? Is it a surprise to you that I am the way I am, even after all this time? It shouldn't be.

Driplets

3031

Down the stairs of our monolithic structure
Past the gas meter and the garbage room
There is a community garden with edibles and compost
6 rocks divided by 2

T in line with the blue stones
D in the vastness of the sky.
T takes left + down the hidden oasis
D holds sharpness + fuzzyness

Plants with prickles | Animal defecation | Trees are shedding bark |
Return

Over the rails
Foliage covers the way
Edges of rocks and wires
To the Playground.

Nature, Rocks, Trees and swings
Bench and Flying Fox
Time resonates within.
There is always somewhere to be.

Would there be a time in our life where we feel like we are not rushing
anymore… A time and place where we just are…

A matrix that we'll bring to life.
I will, We will… The time is NOW.

D, with T.

The Little Changeling:
It Puts in So Little Effort

It lives in such wonderful little worlds, such perfect little worlds that make so little sense. How does it know them so well? How does it explore there, day after week after month after year, and know so little of what we have to show it? Surely it should see the value of returning here; surely it must see why it should listen. Eventually it must see. It came to us, eventually it must take the final steps into our world. The real world, the real places, the real people have so much more to offer it, if only it would come back to us. Surely it knows we would treat it with kindness. Surely it knows we would treat it just as we treat the real children.

We cannot teach what we do not understand. If it will not make itself understood, then that is hardly our fault. We have offered everything we know. If it does not know how to take it, we are hardly to blame. We are trying our hardest—aren't we entitled to our frustrations? Aren't we entitled to tell it how we feel? Honesty is the peak of humanity, after all, and in the end aren't we trying to teach it to be human? It should know, then, exactly where it stands.

No matter our efforts, it drifts further and further from the real children. It ignores them, shuns them, barely reciprocates their acts of charity. How does it expect to become a part of our world when it so rudely turns its back?

Driplets

The Little Changeling: Just Know

You're supposed to just know this. Why don't you know how to do this? You should know better, you're smarter than this—why would you do something like that? Just do it, just know it, you should know what to do, everyone knows what to do. It's so obvious what to do that we shouldn't need to explain it to you. Don't be a smartass, of course you know what to do, stop asking.

Just ask for help. Why do you hate asking for help so much? Why do you have to take on everything that you clearly don't know how to do yourself? It's okay, we're here for you, nobody's going to bite your head off for asking for help. All we want to do is help you Learn.

Don't ask such a stupid question; you should know this already. We already talked about how to do this, you should be able to do this, you're just lazy, and you should know that being lazy is a bad thing because we've already talked about that too. We're glad we had this conversation, now stop being lazy and do the thing that you already know how to do.

Why do you try so hard to predict what we're going to do, what we're going to say, what we're going to think? We don't feel the need to do that, and you shouldn't either. All you need to do is talk to us and we'll tell you, truthfully and honestly, because that's how we do things. You can trust us.

Tell us the truth. Tell us the truth. Tell us the truth. Why aren't you telling us the truth? Stop lying to us; tell us the truth. We know there must be a reason he did what he did, now tell us the truth about what happened. That's not the truth and you know it. Hurry up and just tell us the truth so we can get this over with; these things don't happen for no reason. If you tell us the truth, it will all be okay, but you need to tell us the actual truth. Yes, you keep saying that, but we want you to tell us the truth. Why did you lie about what happened?

You should know that lying is a bad thing, and you should know that if you just tell us the truth, it will all be okay.

Such a good boy. Such a clever boy. Such a nice boy. Such a smart boy. Such a quiet boy. Such a polite boy. Such a well-behaved boy. Look at the potential. Think what you could do. Imagine what life will be like when all of this finally pays off. Imagine what this good clever nice smart quiet polite well-behaved boy is going to do in the world; we'll sit here and cheer you on. You'll be the next big thing. Such a valuable boy. If only you knew how to be one of us. Such a disappointing woman.

You should know how to be human. You should understand what we're talking about. You should have learned all of this already, you're so lazy, you're so stupid, of course we're proud of you, why would you think otherwise?

Driplets

CHAIN STORY:
Pinky, Whizzy & Woolly

They were wearing pink Converse with rainbow laces, a pair of shoes they had had for years and years. Their names were Pinky, Whizzy and Woolly. And they owned a llama farm in the desert. They used their names to indicate their mood, and today they were feeling Whizzy! So they decided to run to the top of the llama field, on the side of a long hill, and lie on the ground and start rolling… Down and down and over and over they rolled. The nearby llamas scattered bleating in alarm, for they were seldom whizzy.

But if there was a day for Whizzy, it was today, as their friend Elvis had rolled into town with his folk-punk band. They were all having a grand old time, dancing into the night, when a giant thunderous roar broke their festivities. It was a giant, menacing Decepticon!

Thankfully, when Elvis had rolled into town, he'd rolled in with Optimus Prime, so the town was saved! But just when everyone was relaxing, Whizzy, who was now feeling a bit Woolly, realised their Converse had disappeared!

"Re-lax, man!" said Elvis.

"I told you before, don't call me *man*", replied Woolly hotly. (They were great mates, but Elvis had a bit to learn.)

"I put them on the Decepticon's feet," Elvis continued, unfazed by the interruption. "He's whizzed off to Oz."

Sam, Jocelyn, Sarah, Urszula, Alex

Live Art Bistro Redux

So
we're going
to see
a
drag performance, and it's
my first time seeing one… My friend is performing. An intimate setting
with people sitting
in chairs waiting for the performances.
And then the performer stands
up from the audience and
removes their human skin,
revealing an alien-reptilian mask. Another
audience member stands up and
peels back their skin, and beneath it is rich, moist, spongy.

A carrot and	sausage cake
is presented.	They begin
to dish	themselves out.
The reptilian	reaches out
its elongated	arms and
passes cake to members	of the audience.

Ze & E.

The Little Changeling: The Mezzanine

I'll show you the school first, because that is where we find the most conflict. Red brick buildings, flat concrete ground, the occasional painted mural for a splash of colour. Very few round shapes, and the only grass is out on the football oval. The dreary construction of the place reflects what is taught here, from dry subject matter into which the teachers could not be putting less effort to values of community (a very specific community of which you are made to feel a part or not, and this status tends to change in only one direction) and of responsibility (individual responsibility for social problems).

It has its nooks and crannies, corners where you can hide from who- or whatever you're hiding from. The library mezzanine is the highest point one can stand in the school, by virtue of being the only room you need to climb not one but two sets of stairs to reach. The librarian would prefer we not go up there, but if we go while she's distracted, she won't know. It is a long room with two long rows of desks and a long whiteboard. If you're walking around, it's easy to make too much noise and be heard from below, but if you like pacing I find the trick is to walk on the desks. It's unusual for anyone to come up here, so if you want to do something undisturbed or use a whiteboard unaccosted, look no further.

It's nice up here.

Driplets

A Conversation between Debbie & Sam

"Debbie, that question makes me a little uncomfortable."

"I'm sorry, Sam, but I have to know! I can't just blab about something like this without knowing where you stand—sorry…"

"To be honest, I don't fully understand it myself. I am still trying to work it out, and it's a little bit difficult. Do you know what I mean?"

"Yeah, I was the same when I first found out as well."

"I know, right? I feel the same way. But I can relate to it. I had similar thoughts when it first happened to me too."

"I think everyone probably does… So… do you want to do it?"

"Yes, I think I do. I know it feels right. I am going to go through with it, but I need your support."

Grace & Jocelyn

DARLING YOU
LOOK SO TIRED
ON THAT BED.
WREST YOUR
HEAD AND
DREAM ONLY
OF PEACEFUL
ANGELS ROCKING
you Gently. Something
I think they can
hold you better than
I can.

I'm not quite sure how
to approach it so
I listen I try hard
to listen but I don't
quite understand.

I know you're trying
mumma bear but
I don't feel heard.
Its not your fold
I know. I just think
were walking
different

tight ropes. We can say
hi turn each others
lure but this is my
path and i stand
by my choices.

The spotlight
illuminates and
they both move to
the own rhythm
of their drum.
Different Beats
with the Same heart.

54

a heart that longs
to love, to dance, to
prance to be accepted
to belong to
cherish to
hold to be present.
Can we at least
agree on that?

yes, I think we

can. Gold radiating
from their hearts
echoing their voices

Sparks of light
flicker and flame
as they embrace
their own paths
all the same.
movement after
movement. sound
after sound. Our
hearts beat as
one to the lone
of the drum.

The lights dim and
curtains close.
They embrace in
a hug and gently,
graciously
   move off
stage.

Sam

It was summer; February or March, when it's the hottest. The streets were filled with people emerging from the comfort of their air-conditioned homes. Streets filled with music were alluring, the thud thud of the bass in sync with heartbeats. Colourful were people flowing along the streets, swaying and flowing with the rhythm. Dancers swishing waves of vibrant fabric. The air hummed with chatter, often punctuated with high-pitched laughter.

When I first stepped out the door to join the river of activity I was still anchored to my mother's hand. "Make sure you stay close so you don't get lost", she warned. I don't remember the moment I detached myself from her. I don't remember intentionally letting go, just the feeling of belonging. My body was meant to move towards being together. It had something to say; it wanted to join in the conversation of dance.

I have always struggled to understand my body. At 50 years of age, I have seen my body change, warp, grow, shrink, tighten, slacken. If my body was charted across time, it would be an abstract line making all kinds of shapes—some wavy and some jagged—going in all sorts of directions. I look down at my body from a head floating above the shoulders. The head is like a buoy bobbing on the surface of water, and the body below sways around randomly with the tide.

The more my cognition grew, the more it outgrew my body. The more the head grew with awareness, the more the body didn't make sense. The head and the body were speaking different languages, but with the head taking the body along for the ride. "Oi!", my body seemed to say. For too long my body was unable to speak, but it is now demanding attention. But who is it speaking to? What is it trying to say?

Grace

Where Did They Notice?

This room floats in its own space—the outside of the building has been lost, unimportant to the breakthrough made inside. The interior looks as corporate as you'll get in a country town, with white walls, office chairs, murky-looking short carpet designed to be cheaply replaced if something were to spill on it, tacky hotel artwork and fluorescent fucking lights, because even a psych's office is incomplete without constantly vibrating bright white light that permeates the soul.

The smiling lady leads the changeling and its human escort down the hallway into a long white room with a long table with wood-grain veneer. The three sit down, the smiling lady continues smiling and the white walls hum with the vibrating white light. The underside of its chair is covered in bumps, the carpet swims with all the creatures that threaten to steal its attention away at any moment and all eyes in the room focus on the little creature. Even the piercing fluorescent lights, buzzing and humming and stabbing and blinding—it even looks at them; anything to avoid the cutting black laser beam eyes and everything behind them.

The smiling lady asks her questions politely, and despite everything it can give its answers as a human should—truthfully and honestly, polite, helpful—and with each answer the smile deepens from one of kindness to one of knowing. Her questions become more direct, in the light she sees all the pieces to be put together, and 15 minutes in she asks the question that feels more like a statement.

The carpet beasties freeze, the vibrating walls huddle in closer, and the changeling looks as closely at the smiling lady's black laser eyes as it can bear. The air to its right thickens, but it dares not try to read the human escort at this of all moments.

Driplets

My Vicarious Splash of Colour

My day-to-day life is fairly run-of-the-mill and ordinary. Nothing interesting really happens to me. I get up, get dressed, have breakfast and ride the tram to work. It's a fairly mundane existence for the most part. In fact, the most interesting part of my life these days is what goes on between the other tram passengers. Particularly that genderqueer pair of friends with the brightly coloured hair.

I don't know their names, and I'm not exactly sure what gender they are. Some days one of them looks like a boy and the other more like a girl, then they might flip things so that the next day it seems like the opposite is true. But they always seem to have their stuff together— they just seem so comfortable in themselves. These days I find myself looking forward to my tram rides, just so I can catch up on what's going on in their lives.

It's usually such a brief encounter though. One of them's already on the tram when I get on and the other jumps on about 15 minutes later. But the first one always gets off just one stop afterwards, so they're only ever together for two to three minutes at the most. But oh, their conversations are just so 'out there' and interesting!

Half the time I don't even know what they're talking about. I'm almost tempted to record them and listen back to their conversations later, so I can make more sense of them. Maybe that would be a bit creepy? I don't know…

Today, the first one's sporting a teal mohawk and rocking rainbow Converse and a rainbow tie-dyed hoodie. I smile at them as I get on, and they smile back. But I feel so bland and colourless compared to them that I can't keep up any eye contact, so I just sit in my seat, get my phone ready to record and read my book to fill in the time.

Before I know it, I see a flash of purple and blue as their friend sweeps past me.

I can't quite hear what they say as they sit down, and I miss the first question by not starting the recording soon enough to catch it. But when the other one gets off the tram, I have something to keep my curious mind turning over all day.

Jocelyn

The Impostor

The room is full of people. Jeans, chinos and check shirts abound in a mass mostly conservatively dressed, chatting about how work has been so busy, so many difficult cases this week, people not paying their bills. Some people are laughing; others are more serious as they take a swig from their glass of beer or wine. Everyone looks like they've just turned up without having to think about what they are wearing or putting on makeup.

You've spent the last hour trying on three different outfits. Too girly, too raunchy, too conservative. Finally you settle on the combo of a sleeveless top and a long print skirt with a pair of heeled boots. You've spent 30 minutes putting on makeup, getting it just right, only to feel right now like it is a strange combination of being both not enough makeup and too much.

You take a deep breath and walk into the room. Will they all stare at you? Will they even notice you? Will anyone talk to you? Will they be surprised, afraid, disgusted? Will they call you by your name?

As you enter the room, more people than you hoped but fewer than you feared turn and stare at you. Do their stares linger a little longer than they need to? Do they recognise you?

Kate

Future Belongings

I'm accompanying a friend to the clinic. They have expressed some uncertainty regarding their gender, and I would like to help them resolve that, however that is to be done. We are waiting for our GP to come in. On the green couch in the nook. I'm holding them to keep them calm. On the chairs up against the walls sit other patients. One of them has arms held tight across their chest. My friend keeps them in sight for a while, hoping to catch eye contact. They wave and say hi.

The stranger notices and gives an uncertain wave back. My friend asks how they're doing and if it's their first time.

"Yes."

In a carefully measured tone—calm but upbeat—my friend says that it's their first time as well. The person smiles and seems to relax a little.

"I've brought a friend with me, for support. This is Ella."

I wave but do not say anything. The other person says hi politely.

"I'm Charlie, by the way."

They say hi again and look away for a moment. "I'm, uh—"

I step in. "You don't have to answer; I know these things can be confronting."

They nod, gratefully.

My friend interjects. "It took me two years to find the right name, and I tried a bunch before I settled."

I chime in. "Don't get attached to names; it only applies pressure. People will accept if you choose one name, then another later on. It's okay."

At this, they relax.

Our doctor enters the room. In a smooth, warm voice, they address us.

"Charlie! Come on through. You're Ella, are you? You too. This way."

They lead us past reception, up the stairs to the left, and into their office. We have a good view of the rooftops.

E. & Charlie

The Room

Kate steps into the room; the sound slaps her in the face as she forges forward, one foot in front of the other in her favourite pair of heel boots. It may have taken an hour to decide what to wear and another hour for her make-up, but these boots needed no decision. These boots were her armour. And fuck, did they make her arse look great. She smiled to herself; the magic of heels. The sound of laughter pulls her back into the moment; she looks around to see where it is coming from. What was so funny? Was it her?

She takes a few more steps forward, looking for a familiar face. Although familiarity isn't the problem. She is looking for a friendly face. Someone who will see her when they look, see her and smile. Instead, as she almost tiptoes in she feels simultaneously invisible and the centre of attention. The energy of the room feels completely jarring, dominant voices piling on top of one another, one-upping each other with how much space they are able to take up. In this room, space isn't given, it isn't shared, it is taken.

Kate finds a chair in the back corner of the room. She sits there quietly, holding her bag tightly on her lap…

Kate

Forest Lights

Thunder. Loud and crackling. Splitting the black afternoon sky in two. Just six days ago it had been blazing hot, the sun beating its rays onto a parched land. The rainy season had announced its arrival with a drop in temperature so fast it took everyone by surprise. Asha gathered the ephedra drying in the yard as fast as she could, creating a makeshift basket with her apron. Piling as high as she could manage, she rushed back to the cottage just in time. Thank goodness. Metra would not have been pleased to have to dry them all over again.

She laid a rug in the main room and spread the twigs to dry out the remaining moisture. *If the air doesn't get too damp, they should be done by tomorrow.* Now for dinner. She turned and made for the kitchen, her socks making no sound as she padded past the bedrooms, through the corridor and down a short flight of stairs. The aroma of lamb stew greeted her as she entered. Metra's favourite. *She's glad she went with her instincts and went for stew despite a warm day.*

This will be her second wet season here. She's getting used to the weather now. The storms were not as violent where she grew up. The weather was milder. Life was still hard, but she had her brothers and sisters, and their parents. She knew she was different from her brothers as a child, preferring the company of her sisters. The villagers thought it was a bit unusual but put it down to childish creativity. Things changed when she got older. People became less tolerant. Worried about the townspeople asking questions, her parents stopped her from managing the stall on market day.

Metra had found her after many moons of wandering, crouched in a hidden corner in the back alleys of Syriah, desperately hiding from the pelting rain, still holding the honey cakes stolen from her earlier. Normally she would have given the kid a beating, but somehow she took pity on her and brought her home. She fed and clothed her, and in time she was able to help out in the kitchen. *Over the years, they have grown closer.* She treated her like a daughter, taught her the ways of her people. She learned about herbs, brews and healing. *Finally, she can begin to align her mind and body.*

The bell jingled as the shop door opened. Metra walked in, wet from the rain, cursing at the sudden downpour.

"Damned rain! Good thing I managed to finish my delivery before it poured," she muttered under her breath. Hearing the door chime, Asha hurried to the front and helped her out of her wet coat. "Sit here by the fire. You'll catch a cold if you're not careful."

The old woman sat at the bench near the stove. Asha brought out two bowls, filled them up with the contents from the pot. They sat down and had their meal, discussing events of the day and planning for the next morning.

"Do we have enough flour for the rest of the month?", asked Metra, sipping her broth silently. Asha winced inwardly. They had run out once a few moons ago, and Metra had made it a point to remind her often.

"I checked. We should have enough for the next two weeks," she replied. She loved the old woman, and was grateful for the life they had together, but she could be irritating at times. "Well, make sure we don't run out," she said, a little too snarkily. She was grumpy today. *Maybe it's the rain.*

"And the herbs?"

"They got rained on a little, but not much. They should be dry tomorrow evening," replied Asha, padding it a little just in case.

They said nothing much after that. Asha knew better than to start a conversation when she was like this. "I can start first tomorrow," she said, offering to give Metra some extra time to rest tomorrow. They took turns starting work in the morning. *The early riser starts the fire in the oven, and measures out the flour and yeast.* She offered to do this every morning, but the old woman would not hear of it, preferring to do her own share. *She can be as stubborn as a mule about some things.*

Meal done, they cleaned up and went to bed.

Cold, cold night. All she had was her nightgown and a thin overcoat. A light sprinkling of snow was starting to build on the ground, her slippers giving her no comfort against the bite. How did she end up here? *And why is she here? Her mind is not responding. Just the compulsion to walk down this path.* Past the trees that grew from skinny saplings to mature trees to the old and gnarled, too wide to wrap her arms around. *Something among the trees beckons to her. She turns right, pushes her way through the brambles, crunching the twigs underfoot.*

There is a light in the distance. Golden and cheerful, like a floating ship of warmth in the cold night, pulling her in. *It grows bigger as she draws near.* Sounds of laughter. The stink of ale. Big and little people bask in the glow, dancing, laughing. *She walks into the light. It's warm here, but there is no fire.*

The people smile at her as they walk past. No-one is surprised. It's as if they are expecting her. A little girl walks up and offers her a flower. She takes it—"Thank you"—and slips it through an embroidery hole in her gown. Over on her right, a crowd sits in front of a shadow play. She sits down too. A young girl beside her smiles shyly and says hello.

There is quite a large crowd gathered. In a darkened corner of the clearing, the cloth screen is illuminated by the backlight. The audience chats silently among themselves as the puppet master settles in and gets ready, arranging his puppets in the right sequence, adjusting the light, taking a sip of water.

The music begins. Woodwinds, cymbals and gongs making strange ethereal sounds. Shadowy hands appear on the screen, dancing in the light, consecrating the performance. She does not know why she knows this. She just does. Black humanlike forms take their place. The story has begun. A peasant girl, a princess, a witch. Eagles, serpents and ogres. Kings, knights and paupers. They all come together in a fantastical tale of love, battle and betrayal.

The peasant girl is caring for her ailing mother. The witch is driven from her village. The princess feels a pull from a longing she can't name. The king has to maintain his authority. The knight does unspeakable deeds in his name and is celebrated. The pauper suffers under the weight of repression. The princess tries to leave. The king finds out and tells his knight to keep her under guard. The peasant girl is desperate to save her mother, but there is nothing she can do. The witch is lost and alone, hiding in the forest, asking why she was cursed with this gift.

Clanking of pots in the distance. *Must be Metra busy in the kitchen.* She looked around. It was still dark. She rubbed her eyes, shook her head slightly to wake up. *Was that a dream?*

Silently she changed out of her sleep clothes and walked to the back. Metra had just started scooping out the flour. She measured the yeast and poured it into the big metal bowl. Taking turns, they mixed the dough and left it to prove. Heating some of the leftover lamb stew, they sat down for breakfast with yesterday's bread.

"Rough night?" Metra asked. It was the first time they had spoken since Asha woke up. *They've settled into a routine over the years.* No conversation until the first break—partly because both were still shaking off their sleep, partly because there was so much to get done. "I heard you mumbling in your sleep."

"Just had a strange dream," replied Asha, stabbing at a piece of meat with her fork. "Nothing exciting."

"Tell me," Metra said, breaking off a piece of bread and dunking it into her bowl, stirring it with a spoon.

"I dreamt I was in the forest. There was some kind of gathering. People were having a good time. That's all."

The stirring stopped momentarily, then continued, slowly. "Sounds like a nice dream."

"Funny thing, though. There was light, but no fire. And it was warm."

The stirring stopped. "That's definitely a dream, then. No such thing as warmth without fire. How's the healing salve going?" Metra said, changing the subject.

Asha grimaced. This was her third attempt this year. *Healing salves are popular, especially now that the days are getting colder.* It started off as a quick relief for joint pain. *But with some experimentation, Metra has improved on the original taught to her by her grandmother, and now it can be used to heal wounds and bruises.* But making the new version had proven difficult for her to master.

Brewing it took some skill and experience, neither of which she had much of at present. "The palm seeds are still fermenting. They'll be ready in three days, I hope."

"Well, make sure to keep it in a warm place. I don't think the top cupboard shelf will do it now that it's cooler. And make sure you have the beeswax ready to go. Timing is critical with this brew."

Asha sighed. "Yeah, I should probably move that someplace warmer." Getting up, she took the jar and placed it in a nook near the stove. Then she walked back and sat down to finish breakfast.

Morning. *The freshly baked loaves are sitting neatly on the shelves. Customers are already starting to come in.* Asha hated dealing with customers. *She is already known in the town, and most people treat her with respect.* Friendly, even. *But it only takes one hater to ruin her day.* Sometimes they would get travellers passing by who were here to get provisions for their journey. She had to deal with stares as they looked her up and down, looking for clues about her gender. *As if wearing a dress isn't enough of an indication. As if having breasts isn't proof enough of her womanhood.*

The scene has changed. The play has taken a darker tone. Shadows cast by puppets, focused at the centre with shadows stretched by the receding light at the edges made more sinister by the tonality of the background percussion. *The puppet master takes on a more sinister tone, intoning dialogue and conflict and bringing the story to the middle phase.*

The princess is making her escape. She managed to deceive the knight and slip away when his attention was elsewhere. *The king discovers this and angrily orders that the knight be beheaded. He sends his ogres out to hunt her down.*

She runs into the forest, in her nightgown and a light jumper and bedroom slippers. Twigs crunched underfoot as she ran. *The king's army is behind her. In her desperate escape, she loses a slipper. Her jumper gets caught in the thorns and gets ripped in places. She sees a light in the distance and runs to it.*

Peasant Girl could not leave her mother. *She hasn't left this place since they buried her that morning. The villagers have left. No-one wants to stay here. They say a witch lives in the woods, and she comes out at night to suck the life out of her unsuspecting victims. Probably a good thing then. Dying seems like a really welcome prospect.* No food. Just some water. *She starts a fire. She needs to mourn.*

She hears sounds of running in the distance. Panting. Coming closer. *Suddenly a woman bursts into the clearing.* Hair in disarray, barefoot and frantic. *Is this the witch?*

Someone's talking. She could hear Metra's voice among them. Strange. *They don't normally have visitors this late at night.* There was light in the main room. Asha tiptoed over to get a closer look. Metra was talking with two men. She had never seen them before. One was bald with a scar on his crown; the other had a thick, black beard and heavy-set eyes. They were all seated on the floor, in a circle, the lamp at the centre making dancing shadows on the walls.

Scar was rubbing his chin, looking worried. "There's been an increase in troop numbers. Our scouts also report an increase in the number of patrols along the border. And just two days ago, we saw several companies of Drakinis along the Xuri Pass."

Asha shivered. *The Drakinis live in the uncharted lands to the south-west, where there is nothing except the parched, swirling sea of sand. Nothing much grows there, which is why many have turned to mercenary work to survive. The less able ones make a living from farming Cyclops Grass and Monango Trees for survival. Others have learned to wrangle the Bawa, fearsome lizard-like creatures with poison in the front and back. They often bring them along for their mercenary work, as they have proven themselves very effective in killing prey.*

BlackBeard grunted, "He hired sorcerers too. We noticed some strange aura over the camps near the castle. Soon we'll be outnumbered. We need your help, Ori."

"I can't, Uri. You know I walked away from that long ago. I appreciate your visits, but I have no wish to go back to all that." Metra's voice was soft but firm. Asha could only just make out her form in the low light, her back turned against her.

"Father's been asking about you," Scar muttered. "Mother is sick. It probably won't be long now. Won't you at least see her one last time? We can work to remove the spell…"

"And to what end?" Metra sighed. "If what you're saying is right, you should save your magic for the clans. You need it more than I do. Besides, she cast it. She can remove it herself."

BlackBeard grunted again. "Hmph. So family doesn't matter to you anymore? I knew marrying a Northerner would come to no good. And where is he now? And what of that…thing you took in? Some sort of redemption?"

"Her name is Asha. She has a name. And she's not an 'it'. And I can look after myself just fine."

Asha had heard enough. She hadn't been referred to in that way in some time. Tears were rolling down her cheeks as she hurried silently back to her bedroom. *It seems like no matter how good she is at potions, no matter how much enchantment she possesses, there is no escaping her birth body. She will never be real. There will always be some part of her that she cannot change, no matter what she does.*

But what if… What if she was better at brews? What if she was more diligent in her training? What if she had had the courage to leave her home village earlier, and…and what? Run into Metra earlier? Maybe she could have ended up dead, or sold to slavery. She knew she was one of the lucky ones. *Not many changed women get to live their lives for very long, if they get to live at all. Most end up dead before reaching their 35th season, many by their own hand. Fewer still get to Change at all. But it doesn't stop her from feeling like her life is nothing but a bad joke.*

Getting into bed, she pulled the covers over herself, and cried herself to sleep.

The puppet master is in a frenzy. The stage is coming to a climactic moment. Peasant Girl stared into the dark, looking for the source of the noise. *Princess bursts through the undergrowth, panting, the look of desperation in her eyes. "Help me!" they seem to be saying.*

She looks at her, bewildered. This can't be the Witch. What is that in the background? The sounds of a million footsteps coming towards her. *The wild woman runs towards her, as if she is able to offer any protection. Then figures slink out of the bushes, illuminated by the firelight.* A hundred hulking beasts, each the size of a bear, bearing horns and clubs, surrounding a runaway princess, a buried woman and a daughter mourning her death.

As the beasts draw closer, they hold each other, lost in their terror. The ogres start grunting in unison, egging each other on and hurrying the ones from behind. It grows louder, until every one of them is grunting in unison, creating a thunderous wall of sound, drowning out any hope of escape.

Except for a hiss from behind. No, from underneath. *The ground shakes momentarily, and slowly, a head emerges. And another. Two serpents slither out of the ground where the grave stands.*

Taken by surprise, the king's army try to run, but it's too late. Surrounding the women, they breathe hellfire on the creatures running away. Out of the corner of her eye, Peasant Girl sees a hooded figure in the background, commanding them.

The bread is in the oven. They are in their second break. They have finished wiping down the shelves. It's still dark out. Sitting at the table with mugs of tea, this is a ritual that they have both come to cherish. The days are normally filled with the business of running the shop, or training. It's at times like this that Metra is not in boss or teacher mode.

"There's unrest in the air," she said. "I get the feeling something is going to happen soon. This war has been going on for too long. Something has to give."

"What do we do?" Asha asked worriedly. She had grown used to the peace and routine of her days. *The prospect of growing conflict and uprooting fills her with dread.* The memory of the conversation she overheard earlier was still fresh in her mind, but she knew better than to bring it up. *Metra can be very private if she wants to be, and this seems to be something she won't want to talk about.*

"We probably should start making preparations," Metra said, taking another sip. "I don't know how things will go, but it doesn't hurt to be prepared."

Night insects gathered around the bulb at the centre of the white screen. *A large banana trunk sits at the bottom, holding it taut.* Flat figurines with sticks made from bamboo, standing upright in a row on either side. *At the centre, a small man with a headdress sits cross-legged, wearing a sarong and khaki pants.*

She isn't sure what story he is telling tonight. She's just mesmerised by the movements and hand gestures made in the light, intonations and words hypnotically making her lose track of time. In time, the performance is over, and she is suddenly aware of the man sitting in front of her, a stump of smoking cigarette in his mouth, watching as if waiting for her to wake up from her stupor. All is quiet save for the high-pitched buzzing of cicadas in the background. The band had stopped playing and had already left. *It's just the two of them.*

He sits there, saying nothing.

After what seems an interminably long time, she asks, "Who are you?"

"They call me Tok Dalang. I am the puppet master. Do you know why you are here?" The man was quiet and gentle.

"I… Well…" Asha mumbled incoherently. "Uh… Where am I?"

"You are in the stage hut," said Tok Dalang, not really answering her question at all. "Behind the veil."

"Why do I keep coming back here?"

"We only revisit places we run away from," said the old man, taking a drag from his cigarette, "and you have been running for a long time, young one." *He stubs his cigarette in his ashtray, then leans forward and looks at her, his gentle eyes meeting hers.* "You feel it, don't you? When you get angry. Or afraid. How you have to keep it down, every time."

Tok Dalang shifted his posture. "It will only get stronger. There's only so much you can do to suppress who you are. You have to embrace it, or it will devour you."

The crash intruded into her dream world, bringing her back to the bedroom. Was it from the dream? Another crash, then another. *No, this is real.* Alarmed, she got out of bed and rushed to the main room.

Asha stood still, horrified. *What is this creature?* Standing in the room, framed by the black hole where the wall had been, framed by the yellow light of the fireplace, stood a monster the size of a small house. Head of a serpent, body of an armoured ox, and a tail with a spiked club at the end. Metra was on the ground beside her, bloodied, knocked unconscious by a chunk of wall that had burst from behind.

The creature let out a bellow so loud it made her head spin and nearly knocked her to the ground. It took a step forward and swung its tail again, making the black hole even bigger. The thundering crash brought Asha back to her senses. It made for Metra, her prone body unmoving. All Asha wanted was to run away, but she couldn't. She couldn't leave the one person who took care of her when no-one else would. This was her home, and this foul creature was destroying it. No. *This intruder must leave. Her fear is replaced by a quiet, calm determination, a knowing that she can repel this beast.* Something built up inside her; all that anger channelled into a ball of energy that she unleashed into—

Out of nowhere, a faint form of yellow light appeared in front of her, slowly solidifying into outlines, then increasing in form and solidifying until it became an equally fearsome creature made of light. The light faded and the creature took form, now a walking tank with four legs, now a leather-clad animal with enormous hoofs, now an armoured, three-horned rhinoceros breathing fire. It charged at the creature, head down, and stabbed it in the neck, driving it out to the courtyard. The scales were too thick for the horn to make purchase. The creature screamed, raised its tail and prepared to swing the club. But the rhino was prepared and was already following up its lunge with fire. Rearing its head, it heaved a torrent of flames hot enough to burn through the serpent's scales. Taken by surprise, the creature reared up, then fell on its back, dying. The rain of fire continued until the serpent was still. Rhino stopped, stood still for a moment, then started glowing. Lines of light took its place, then slowly faded, erased by the blackness of the night.

Asha was spent. Knees weak, she dropped down to the floor. Fatigue, fear, elation and relief fighting for attention. Where did that come from? *Am I some kind of monster?* She stayed on the ground for a long while, too exhausted to move.

Finally she got up. Slowly, she stumbled across to her guardian. Metra was barely moving.

"Metra! Are you okay?" she said softly, knowing that the end was near.

Her breathing was laboured. A chunk of wall had fallen on her when the club-tailed creature broke in, breaking her ribs and possibly puncturing her lungs. The melee had dislodged it, saving Asha from removing it.

"It's too late, my child… My end is near," Metra half whispered to the daughter she never had. Asha moved closer, desperate to hear what might be her last, dying words.

"There is so much I should have told you. I thought you were not ready. Now I know I waited too long." Metra coughed, blood spitting out as she did so. Asha looked on desperately, knowing she needed to turn her on her side to prevent her drowning, but also knowing that with her crushed ribs, it would kill her anyway.

"Go to Uri. My bedroom. The envelope. The answer's there…"

Those were the last words she spoke. There was nothing to accompany the screaming silence except the black sky and the dying embers in the fireplace. Asha bent down and hugged the dead body, desperately willing her to come back. She was too shocked to even cry.

Many moments later, she willed herself back up. *Get a grip, Asha. Someone will come soon, and questions will be asked. And you will likely be seen as the perpetrator.* And, as she had learned from her past, the only way to safety was to disappear.

Slowly, she got up and went to Metra's bedroom. She opened the drawer in the bedside table and found an envelope, sealed with wax and an indecipherable stamp. *No time to think. Move.* Next, she walked back to her bedroom one last time, to pack her things. Then she went to the kitchen, grabbed a loaf of bread, wrapped it in a piece of cloth, stepped out of the house and walked away.

Sarah

Title image: Juho Luomala. Images-in-text: tree, png.is; Wayang, vecteezy.com; bread, rattanachomphoo, www.freepik.com; Naka, gograph.com

My Translucent Thumbnails

I'd done something naughty. No-one was going to know—probably. Hopefully! I was scared of someone noticing, but at the same time curious what would happen if they did. It wasn't a big deal, really. But if anyone noticed, the teasing might start again, and I'd gotten used to not having to worry about that.

Slowly, carefully, when I was sure no-one else was watching, I opened the fist I'd made on my left hand.

I gasped.

I could see it!

My thumb with its coating of nail gleamer!

It was shiny, reflecting the fluorescent lights above me.

No-one could see it but me.

Most people were sitting like me, with their heads bent over their workbooks and not looking at anyone else. I felt safe like that. I was in my own protected bubble.

I looked at my shiny thumbnail again and rubbed my right pointer finger over it. It felt slick and smooth and different.

I heard movement and looked up to see the teacher walking around the room. I quickly slipped my thumb back inside a fist. She hadn't seen. I was safe again.

I still don't know what made me put it on, but knowing it was there made my heart beat faster. It was kind of exciting! There was something about me that no-one else knew and no-one else expected. Only I knew it, and it was exciting to have that secret knowledge that I could share with someone in an instant and they might not even notice that I'd done it.

It gave me such a thrill that when I went home, I snuck into my sister's room and put a coat of gleamer on my other thumb. It was going to be harder to hide it on both hands now, so I was taking a bit of a risk, but I almost wanted someone to notice. I wanted to know what they'd say to me or what they'd say about me. Would I be a deviant freak, or would I be someone just trying to get attention?

That was the thing—I think I WAS trying to get attention. I was making it harder to hide and easier to get caught.

The next morning I was sitting in class, writing with my head bent over my desk again when the teacher started walking around checking on us to see how we were going with our work. She must have noticed my shiny thumb. I couldn't hide it! It reflected the overhead lights back at me as my hand moved across my page. She had to have seen it!

But she never said anything. Did she notice?

Did she feel sorry for me?

Did she think I was some poor little queer boy who needed to be protected?

Was she secretly proud of my tiny, insignificant act of rebellion?

I knew it was an act of rebellion. I'd learned a few years before that boys had to stick to boy-like behaviour or else they would be punished.

And I'd followed the rules as best as I could, but I still needed something that was me, even if no-one else would know but me.

A few days later, one of the girls in my class must have noticed, because she asked me, "Are you wearing nail polish?". And for some reason I forgot all about self-preservation as my need to correct her took over. So I said, "No, it's not nail polish, it's a gleamer," and then immediately focused back on my work. She didn't say anything else, and nobody else ever mentioned it, so I felt like I'd gotten away with something. My one little moment of gender non-conforming rebellion, wearing translucent nail gleamer on my thumbs.

Jocelyn

About this piece:
Jocelyn: I wrote this in response to a poem Sarah read out about her own moment of rebellion with a single painted fingernail—it triggered this memory for me. I was moved by the similarity of our experience of this tiny, almost insignificant thing: that two people who felt alone in that moment in their lives, in different times and in different parts of the world even, could find comfort in doing this simple thing for themselves. It was reassuring to me to know that I wasn't a bit of a freak in that moment but that someone else could find comfort in the same act. It has actually made me feel more confident in myself to feel connected to someone in this way—by this tiny, individual action.

Sarah: I was in a very dark place. I had just come out to my partner a few weeks earlier, after enduring months of heavy, excruciating dysphoria after my egg cracked. Someone once said to keep that one little thing, so that if there's nothing else, you still have something to hold on to. *This is my connection to me. To her.* I was so terrified of letting anyone know, including myself, that I made sure that it was the most inconspicuous thing I could have: transparent polish on my left pinkie.

And so it was that I found myself in a bus, on my daily commute, tapping out a poem on my mobile phone:

> There's nail polish on my pinky
> I wear it every day
> I wear it with a clear finish
> To let me know I am this way
>
> There's nail polish on my finger
> It helps me assuage the hunger
> It is my very own personal secret
> In an otherwise barren desert
>
> In that finger is little Sarah, I think
> You will miss her if you blink
> For who, or what, am I exactly?
> Please excuse me while I check my reality

I would secretly rub my fourth finger on my nail, just to feel its smoothness… I still do, after starting my transition, so many years later. It's not so much a thrill as it gives me a connection to who I am…that forbidden part that would be shamed and bullied if she ever came out.

Perhaps it's this connection that maintained my sanity the whole time. In the bus, rushing through the hot summer rain, sweaty office workers rushing home. At work, cold office air blowing down my back. In a meeting, discussing project deadlines and fighting with management. Always there. Giving comfort.

Jocelyn: Yeah, I know what you mean—it's the connection of my past, confused, naive self to who I am now in my present gender transition journey that makes this story significant. I paint my nails all the time now, as colourfully as I can, and it has become an important part of my self-expression.

Sarah: I remember one day, it was the monsoon. I was on Orchard MRT, boarding the train to go home. Just three stops. But in conservative Singapore, this was terrifying. Holding the handrails, making sure it's my right hand. Hoping the wetness of my hands would mask the shine on my finger.

Jocelyn: I guess other people could find that terror insignificant over such a small thing, but I remember how significant it felt to me at the time. I was terrified of someone seeing it, whilst at the same time I wanted to let that side of myself show, even just a little bit. And through the anxiety and terror, it was almost exhilarating.

Sarah: Yes. Likely no-one noticed. Doing this on your own can be so hard. But it's gratifying to know that there are actually organisations that support trans people now.

Jocelyn: I'm not sure I'd understand myself the way I do now without the kind of support I've received from those I've met online, who have worked through this before me. It's probably why I didn't recognise my trans-ness when I was younger—I just didn't have the tools to understand it, so I kept it hidden even from myself.

Sarah: I kept it down for so long… I didn't transition until it was a do-or-die option.

One memory I had was around five years ago. I was driving with a friend to pick up a birthday cake. Julia Kaye had just come out and was starting to publish her comic strips. We were in a dark alley where I had parked my car. She walked into the shop and I followed behind, staring at the phone. I saw her comic strip, turned off the phone and said silently to myself, "Don't go there". Meanwhile, the whole time, despite myself, I kept that nail polish on my fingernail. Rubbing the smooth surface brought me a sense of comfort I could not articulate.

Jocelyn: My subconscious denial reflex is super strong, so I didn't even have those sorts of moments in my past. Sometimes I wish I had, because then I'd feel like I understand myself better now. But instead, my transition journey is full of self-discovery. It leaves me feeling like I'm in a state of flux, exploring what I can and discovering how I like to present myself.

It feels like I came to understand who I really am slowly over the last several months, starting off by coming out as non-binary. Gradually, as I added more feminine styles to my presentation, I started feeling more and more comfortable. Who I am now just feels overwhelmingly right in a way I've never experienced before. It's like my true self is this mystery that I'm gradually solving, one clue at a time.

Sarah: It's a journey. There's the pushback we get from the external world, coming out, wondering if someone will accept us. But the greatest hurdle we face is us. They say when you're trans, the biggest transphobe you'll meet is yourself. My biggest struggles are with my own acceptance of who I am. That's why pride matters. It's not just about having fun. It's celebrating who we are and how we are still here and thriving despite living in a world that is still struggling to accept us.

Queering the Map: My Doctor's Office

My doctor's office. The place that I first sat, sobbed and felt heard. The place where no-one asked questions like: 'Are you sure?' *(Yes I think so)* or 'How do you know?' *(I don't know how I know, I just do).*

Instead, I was asked the questions that mattered: how I wanted to be myself, how I wanted to get my hands on the sweet, bittersweet elixir of second puberty.

The first time that I wanted to book my next appointment. Going with what's right, 100 kilometres an hour down the highway of my gender journey.

The rush and exhilaration of being me, learning more about myself with every bit of professional advice. The dots in my map get connected more and more with each visit. How to get from point A to B, or the closest rest stop in the meantime.

It all began in the waiting room of that clinic, when I felt seen and heard. When they let me have the title of 'Mr' even though, back then, it wasn't legally so.

Marley

Dion

Playing dress-ups with my Grandma was my escape. She let me go into her wardrobe and try on her majestic gowns that she used to go to town in. Sometimes I'd sit there and run my hands over her make-up case. She'd sit down and say, "Go on bub, make me look like a superstar. This is just between you and me". I'd walk slowly alongside her wardrobe, feeling the textures of the fabric under my fingertips, and this longing and yearning that was so profound was finally calmed. This was home; it both thrilled me and scared the shit out of me. Her joy and 'I give not a single fuck' attitude was the antidote to that anxiety that lived in my spine on the daily. Don't give it up, Dion, don't let them see you.

Since Nan was gone it had all turned to shit, I closed that door, pushed it down so far and deep that you'd never have known it even existed.

Until one night, it's like the portal opened again.

◆◇◆

"Dion! Hey, what's up man, what are you doing here?" It was Bonita from school. Woah, she, they, looked different. "Oh hey! What's up?" I gave them a squeeze. "How have you been sis?" Their face dropped, and they noticeably shifted their energy. "I'm so sorry, what should I call you now?" They smiled. "Call me Ben." Ben squeezed my hand. "Oi, what are you up to? Come here, I want to show you something."

Down an alleyway there was a loud, rolling bass hum spreading out to the street. A thick layer of ciggy smoke haloed around the gang we approached. That thick bass is pulsating again as we push open the door to the club. A wall of sound and sensory overload. The claps accentuate the air. I see people dropping low and grinding their way up on their partners. A dense haze filters through the air as UV catches the light on patterned sections of my outfit. And then I glimpse her. HER.

She's a walking, sculptural masterpiece, encased in luminescent bionic fluid. Face painted for the gods. Backlit by a beaming light. I can only see the outline of your eyes and teeth and the silhouette of that afro, backlit in all its masterful glory. She is a god.

Who is she? She is freedom, she is otherworldly, she is the embodiment of femininity reconfigured, refined, re-imagined; what is it to be her? As we lock eyes, as we pass in the club, I slow down; I'm eclipsed by her beauty. Do I desire her? Do I desire to be her? Fuck.

◆◇◆

"Dion, when are you going to bring home a wife eh?" My aunty squeezes my cheek hard. "I'm concentrating on my studies, Aunty." Cue eyeroll and loitering over the food table, trying to occupy my attention by proceeding to eat my weight in coconut rice to avoid being accosted again.

We live for these moments.

◆◇◆

If I don't exist, how will I leave a shadow? Fuck my life has been a shit-show, but whose hasn't? Nothing like being gay, black and trans?? OMG I feel like such a freak. I think a lot of times I feel like I'm not here. Like not really here. As in, there's not a place for me, you know? Like there's not even a fucking toilet for me? How can I exist in defiance of everything that's normal (gender, race bla bla bla), but yet not exist at all to the world. People always tell you where they don't want you. The fucking toilets, change rooms, public spaces, school…but they don't say, 'Here, this is a space for you'. And people wonder why we have such a disrupted sense of belonging.

On the flip side, maybe that shit is freeing. Maybe my existence or lack thereof is what makes me free. I don't have to conform to this life, or structure or rules. I make my own rules, or our community make our rules. But this world isn't shadowless, patriarchy isn't shadowless, colonialism isn't shadowless—we are living in the shadow of its impact. We are in that shadow, and it has changed us, yet our shadows haven't made an impact yet. We don't matter? It's funny how this idea of disappearing and being nothing is both terrifying, sad and freeing.

What is shadowless? Is that not impact? Is that illumination? It's midnight, with clouds, and perfectly dappled lighting across the sky. Is it liberation when shadows are gone, no longer have to be inhabited?

It's confronting to see who turns towards me, and who turns away at this time.

◄◊►

OMG

My feet grounding again with the pulse as we move further into the night.

Ripley

Random Scary Dance

I'm no less the stage
than the stage is me
I'm no less the stage than anyone.
It's exhilarating
—the constant movement.
Watching it back, I can see myself smile.
So satisfied the other night—him.
I'm not like that for others,
only for him.
Maybe it's the spinning dance,
weaving a thread.
A dance story,
a love story.
I love that story.
But I wonder…
wait, scary
dark baseline that vibrates through the tip.
I trip?
If I fall—
I could be a man because what have I got left?
I could do a man because what have I got to lose?
I'm much more drawn into them now.
Yet, now my steps aren't choreographed by other people,
being a bro? scary scary
The surface is easy in the dance of a man.
Yet deeply, truly…
Well, what am I? So queer. It brings me too-toos.
My too-toos bring all the boys to the yard.
I feel dysphoric in my way through life.
Not just someone else's body
but someone else's life.

What if I too, am untrue?

Maybe my housemate has a point.

Maybe I need pointe shoes.

Contort myself into my dreams.

If I commit to how I want to live

will I commit myself to madness?

I'm not sure I am my parent's reaction

to their own pain.

But I'm not sure I'm not.

I loved the dress billowing out as I stepped onto that scary stage.

I could just be.

I could just relate.

Irrelevant of relatives

—I feel, I fall, I only want one floor.

I came, I saw, I conquered the gasping core.

The air captured the dust as a twirl

as I exhaled.

I dance with this and also… I am not this?

Maybe I'm not…relaxed.

How does anyone ever relax?

It is a complement, it is overwhelming, it is through the world,

spinning my way through time from when I was little,

that video a pirouette to the present.

Will I break a bone?

I couldn't find the exit to the dance

but I didn't mind.

So please, don't act for me,

just reject me.

Only give me what is true.

Do I?

I think it's me

I think I'm the one the others are scared of.

Lewin

Whispers in the Water

Verse 1
We are the whispers in the water, the heartbreak at the border
The long glance at the harbour, the fire in our eyes

We are the whispers in the water, the heartbreak at the border
The barista who knows your order, the fire that never dies

Bridge
I feel it when we dance, a taste of what could be
You may say I'm a dreamer, but I dream of being free
I feel it when we dance, a taste of what could be
You may say I'm a dreamer, but I dream of being free
Oh!

Verse 2
We're the siblings of forgiven wrongs, the keepers of forgotten songs
The watchers of the waterways, the flirts over crochet

We're sons of storms like Hercules, the hum between the harmonies
The unrevised histories, the body's invisible mysteries

We're the daughters of the deities, who don't remember what day it is
With their fingers on the pulse of life, a skip in their stride of pride

We're the children of the waterfalls, the hope inside the pay phone calls
The midwives of the winter balls, the secret of the bride

Bridge
I feel it when we dance, a taste of what could be
You may say I'm a dreamer, but I dream of being free

I feel it when we dance, a taste of what could be
You may say I'm a dreamer, but I dream of being free
Oh!

Verse 3
They can take our labour, but they can never take our fire
Remember there is nothing wrong, with our queer desire

We can feel when we kiss, the sacred on our lips
The wonder in our wild hearts, the waves between our hips

The joy of walking hand in hand, the friend who knows all ya mad plans
Fireplace in the facebook groups, the keepers of the chicken coops

We're knowing it will be alright, the lift home from a wild night
The love that dares to speak its name, we dare to speak its name

Bridge
I feel it when we dance, a taste of what could be
You may say I'm a dreamer, but I dream of being free
I feel it when we dance, a taste of what could be
You may say I'm a dreamer, but I dream of being free

Lewin

In front of you is a river.

An old river. You can see the bottom lined with pebbles and rocks. The water sits so still at the bottom. As if it isn't moving. You can also see some fish in the water. Beneath the surface, following the current. The top of the water contrasts with what is underneath. At some points, the water is still and you can see no tension.

But where the rocks are larger and reach up around the water's surface there is a brisk flow, accompanied by the white spray. You can't help but notice that this feels static. Despite the constant movement and shifting of the water itself, the portion of river in front of you feels as though it is not moving. The incoming water bounces off the rocks in the same way. The water underneath does not disrupt the pebbles or the fish, even though it too is moving as the current. The fish swim and leave, but more fish arrive to take their place.

This scene, this part of the river that you are staring at, does not appear to change. It is moving with the ambience of nature, yes, but a picture now would look the same as a picture tomorrow. But you know that this isn't true. Because each element, each molecule of water is different to the one that came before it. Every time the water flows with the current of the river it is anew.

Beside you a tree is dropping its leaves. The seasons are changing. It is getting colder. And so the leaves are dying. And falling. They are all around you on the ground. You pick one up. It's mostly yellow, but there is still a twinge of green around the edge. Its destiny was to fall from the tree and become a part of the Earth. It would live and die in this scene. But not now. You have decided to change its fate.

Getting up from your spot on the ground you move closer to the river's edge. The water is shallow at this point. The pebbles are clearer. But within reach is a large rock. It is sticking up out of the water, beyond it a flurry of atoms being pushed around by a larger force. You take a step over the shallow water and onto the rock. It is firm in the ground. Your other foot meets to join the first and you are now allowing your body to exist in this new state. Below you the water still rushes, and you bend down to touch it gently. It's cold, but pleasantly so. It rushes around your fingers until you pull back. The river has left its mark on you, even though it will fade. Crouching down to pull yourself closer, you reach out your hand with the leaf, hovering it above the busy water. You take a breath. Then you let go.

The leaf floats down slowly in comparison to the speed at which the river rushes it away from you. It moves along the water with urgency, pulled away to continue its journey beyond what you can see. It is gone. And now you understand. Nothing is the same as what was before it. But it's also not entirely different.

Charlie

THE ONGOING RIVER

SELF

AN ONGOING RIVER SELF. AN ONGOING PROCESS, NEVER ENDING, NEVER TELLING. JUST BECOMING, BECOMING ALL THE POSSIBILITIES YOU DREAM OF AND ALL THAT YOU CAN SEE AND FEEL. IT ALL LIES ON THE ONGOING RIVER SELF. SPLISH, SPLOSH, SPASH. ROCKS CRAWL IN, FROGS HOP ABOUT ALL ALONG THE RIVER SELF. A PLACE THAT CAN GET POLLUTED AT TIMES. A PLACE THAT REFLECTS THE STARS AND THE MOON. A PLACE THAT EMBRACES THE ONGOING FLOW OF LIFE. A SANCTUARY AMONG OTHER SANCTUARIES. A PLACE TO CALL YOUR OWN. FLOW UP. FLOW DOWN. FLOW ALL AROUND. THE ONGOING RIVER SELF.

Journey + River

All-encompassing parts of existing.

Between human and nature, the point of cohesion.

The courage of shaping a unique transformation flowing through the blood and tears of us all.

All-encompassing, we are here.

Directionless and scared…

Realising we are what is needed.

Rising.

D

ONLY YOU AND YOU ALONE CAN CHANGE YOUR SITUATION. Leonardo DiCaprio

Nothing worth doing is worth doing it alone

HOW DO I WANT TO FEEL THIS WEEK

GRATEFUL FOR   HABITS   M T W T F S S No

GOAL   O O O O O O O

WEEKLY WINS   O O O O O O O

                                                         O O O O O O O

                                                         O O O O O O O

                                                         O O O O O O O

I'm floating down...

...and I don't know where I'm going to end up, but I don't need to know where this water ends when all I need to do is step in. The current is taking me somewhere whether I like it or not, and what will happen if I fight it? More frighteningly, what will happen if I follow it? Do I relax? Do I panic? How do I know how to feel? How do I know what to do? How do I know what I'm supposed to be learning? How do I know what I'm supposed to be taught? How do I know who I will meet, and how do I know how to leave them better than I found them? Words are all I can bring with me, but how much more am I leaving behind? Will anyone join me in this water, or are you all too busy with your own? Will I join anyone else in their rapids, or am I too busy trying to teach myself how to swim? How do you learn to swim? Where did you people get boats from? Just get in your boat, what are you doing? Why wouldn't you just make it easier on yourself and get on board? No, of course you can't come on board mine; that would be ridiculous.

Driplets

Alien Tea Party (I)

A cold touch hit her skin. The water poured from the tap like blasting water pipes bursting at the seams. She couldn't go out there. Not again. She was a they. They did not exist in the space created around them, so she was a her. A her that existed in a realm of he and him. No 'they' allowed. 'No they allowed' might as well have been posted on the outside cubicles. On the front of the building. On the foreheads of those she came in contact with. She, they, he. What did it matter? After a while she wiped her face with the water. Splashing it down their arms. Those arms. My arms. My touch. My body. My being. So what if they don't understand? So what if they don't see me for how I see myself? Does it matter when I don't know these people? Does it matter when they don't need to know me? I don't know. I don't have the answers for this. So yes I will stay masked. I will wear my gold shield of protection. My invisibility cloak. My imagination is the only thing they cannot take from me. My imagination is the only thing I can project into this space without creating some sort of confusion. I imagine sparkling gender-diverse creatures. Joining us at the tables. Sitting with us. Creatures that have come from galaxies to be here. For this event. Unfortunately the others can't see but I can. Perhaps only the gender diverse can. I wink and laugh at one of the creatures. They pull a silly face at me and then to the person sitting across from them who was oblivious to any sort of extraordinary terrestrial activity. Who knows what my mind is thinking, but I know that thinking and imagining brings me great comfort in a world where I don't see myself reflected. In a world that holds barriers to what I can, what we can, be. I decide to be the creator of my universe. I decide to choose creatures, cuddly, fluffy, scaly, scrubby and scatty. All sorts of shapes and sizes welcome. Any planet, any creature may sit at our tables and enjoy meals at this tea party. A small pink fluff-ball jumps on my lap and makes a squeal of joy. I raise my hand in fright and then settle when they shoot me a big smile. I land my hand on their head and pat. Pat pat pat. Little friend of the universe. How nice of you to come join this party when I was feeling so lonely. I don't feel so lonely anymore. I don't feel like I'm not seen or heard, because I've created a party of my own. A parallel party you might say. We can have a gender-diverse, aliens-welcome party that coexists simultaneously with this cisgendered party. Sure they have cheese and wine, but we have swirly glitter balls that make your tongue purple and your eyes red. Sure they have suits and dresses, but we got outfits that make us shine and textures that exceed gravity.

Ze

Beatrix (Bea):
Interview with a Witch

What's your favourite childhood memory?
I remember when I was a kid there was this time when I was talking really passionately about something, I couldn't tell you what about, but I remember both of my parents just staring at me with interest one minute, and the next they were shocked and a little confused. I had no idea what was going on, because I wasn't doing anything different to what I would normally do, but somehow they just couldn't stop staring at me. When I eventually got them to explain what was going on they told me that my eyes had dramatically changed colour from their usual brown to bright purple. They were both so excited, because that was the first time I showed signs of having magic in me. I was also excited, but it's also one of the only times I've ever seen both my parents genuinely shocked about something, and I find that really amusing.

Who do you respect the most, and why?
I have a friend, Misty, who is half-siren, and she is the most amazing person I've ever met. Every other half-siren I've met has been shy and not spoken much, because their voice has an effect on the people around them. But my friend decided to find a way to make her voice less impactful so that she could feel more comfortable talking to people. Now she doesn't ever shut up, because she can turn her ability on and off at will. It's pretty incredible.

What makes you laugh?
Hmmm. This one is a hard one to answer, because I will laugh at the weirdest things sometimes. I'm gonna say Misty, because she's a pretty funny person. But she thinks I'm way funnier than her and I don't get it. I think maybe she just gets amusement out of me being gullible and a

little spacey. But I really enjoy it when she tells a funny story, because she is so animated!

How do you feel about your looks? Describe yourself.
I'm pretty comfortable with how I look now. It took a long time for me to get to this point though. I look mostly human, but I have little lightning-bolt-looking lines all over my body. They're blue and just exist on my skin like tattoos do. I actually got a little storm cloud tattoo on the back of my neck to match. I like my eyes, because they change colours all the time. Except they do so depending on my mood, so I can't really hide anything. Aside from that I look pretty much human. My hair is half black, half white at the moment and is short and fluffy. It kinda sits on the top of my head like a cloud. So yeah, I'm pretty happy with the way I look. Even if it's a tad too feminine for my liking sometimes.

How old are you?
Uh, late twenties. I don't really wanna share my specific age, 'cause I know there are a few dark magic potions that can use your age against you.

What three adjectives best describe you?
Oh, this is tricky. An open book? As in I am pretty easy to read, in part because of my eyes, but I also just don't feel the need to hide my thoughts. Friendly. I will talk to almost anyone. If you're a dick then maybe not, but I always give people a chance. And maybe a bit creative? I'm always looking for new ways to create potions or use my powers. Usually I just want shortcuts to be fair though. *laughs*

Do you see your parents regularly?
Not really. They live quite far from me. I also don't really get along with them much anymore. They're not really fond of how I live my life. At this point they don't say much about it, 'cause they've worked out they can't stop me from doing whatever I want. But I'd still rather not deal with their disapproving looks and bites of sarcasm. So I see them maybe twice a year. If they've been nice.

About Beatrix:

Bea is non-binary (they/them) and is half-human, half-witch. When they were born their parents didn't know which parent they were going to take after, as they were born as any human/witch is. For the first 12-ish years of their life there was no indication that they were anything but human. Then they started to show physical signs of their magic: their eyes would change colours with their mood, their skin started to show lines that looked somewhat like veins, only thinner and jagged like lightning bolts. It took time to master the new skills that were thrust upon them, but as they grew older they were able to control small pockets of weather, conjure small sprites to target magic at, and they learned how to make potions.

Charlie

Orrin:
Interview with a Dragon

What's your favourite childhood memory?
My favourite childhood memory is the first time I flew. I believe it was at school, a warm day in summer at the playground. I tried doing a pull-up to show off to my friends; some of them chuckled at me and others didn't believe I could do it. Some others cheered me on. The more I tried to huff and heave, the more my dragon wings flapped and my eyes squinted, the quicker I lifted off the ground. I was still holding the playground bars, but it was the first time I had actually used my wings at that height.* Now I can do that sort of motion with no effort, but because it was a first, it was important to me.

Who do you respect the most, and why?
Hmmm…. This one would be tough. It's hard to think of. Let's see, perhaps the people I respect are the most open-minded, the fun, the kind. It's difficult to pinpoint an individual over qualities that one admires in a person.

What makes you laugh?
There are a lot of things that make me laugh, many of them just the little things. Like when glitter gets on my nose, or if I do something clumsy. You can laugh at almost anything when you find the good nature in it. My favourite is bad fire puns. It seems a bit predictable since I'm part-dragon. The best one I've ever heard would have to be: 'I want to make a really long, bad lizard joke… But I don't want to let it dragon.'

Get it? Drag-on. That one always makes me laugh, no matter what sort of day I've had.

How do you feel about your looks? Describe yourself.

I have long hair; it's a dark colour. My eyes are rather bright, a sort of blueish-greenish that matches with the seasons and the colour of my wings. I've got a fair bit of stature, quite tall but not for a part-dragon. My wings are longer than my arms. I think they go to about…six foot in span? Most say I've got a sharp face, chin, jawline and all that. My most favourite thing would be the tattoos. I got them when I was old enough to, and I love that the colour of the ink matches perfectly. The compass stands for direction. Of course it does! There's some flowers and another style map. I might not be the tallest or strongest out there, but I've grown into myself, and I think that's important.

How old are you?

How old do you think I am?** What calendar are we following here? It all depends on who's asking and where they're asking and why they're asking, doesn't it? But if you simply must know… Hmmm, no. Too many specifics.

*What three adjectives*** best describe you?*

I am relaxed (most of the time), passionate (because I'm a dragon, and that's what we're known for) and I would like to say intellectual, because I've started to hoard books and I quite like reading them. Now, there is a little irony in that, because dragons and libraries aren't known to get along very well.

Do you see your parents regularly?

I do, yeah. My dad is also a part-dragon like me, though his colours are more in the expected dragon colours. Reds, golds. We have some fun family dinners.**** My other dad likes to roll his eyes and make jokes that we need to put our wings away at the table. He's human and where I get my love of books from. He also makes the best soups, especially tomato soup with extra basil.

About Orrin:

When his wings grew in, it surprised everyone. Both of his dads were happy about his powerful dragon wings, though they usually took other people by surprise. He was a little small when they grew in, so once they got big and heavy, it was a struggle not to fall over. They drape by his ankles now and he wears them with a lot of pride, which was something he had to work through. He wasn't always the confident, heroic or strong leader; it took work to get there. Because he had been small and scrawny, they expected his wings to be the same.

Unfortunately for them, they had misjudged.

It took time for him to be able to be heard and even longer to be able to control the fire that tried to burst through his nostrils. Through the expectations of the world around him, he instead became a bit of a helping hand.

Orrin is a bit like people we see in our world all the time; they often grow up in a way we don't expect: fabulous and unique!

Marley

* Dragon flight takes a lot of skill and practice. Orrin had trained with his father a little bit before that. They weren't the more spiny wings that they expected, the ones typically formed by people who looked like him. They were big, grand and powerful, and although the colour was different, his wings looked exactly like his father's.
** Dragons get a bit spiny about ages. Different people use different calendars, so their sense of time differs a little.
*** Reducing people to adjectives is hard enough, let alone 100-year-old draconic teenagers!
**** Family dinners are tough if you have wings and tails getting in the way of cutlery— a good thing to note for draconic guests.

The Perpetual Gendered Bathroom Decision

You're a cis male—in other words, you were assigned 'male' at birth—and you've never questioned this, always confident in your identification, to the point that you don't even consciously think about it.

You've just arrived in a new city by train, to visit a friend. You've texted them to let them know you're here, and they'll be here to pick you up in about 10 minutes. You've been cooped up in that carriage all day and you really need to pee.

You see a sign that looks like it points to the women's toilet, so you look around for the sign for the men's, but you can't see one anywhere.

A worker in railways uniform is standing a few metres away looking at their phone, so you approach her and ask where the toilets are. She looks at you as if you're a bit dense, points in the direction you've just come from, towards the ladies', and says, "They're just over there, right where the sign says 'Toilets'".

You feel a bit embarrassed by their assumption that you're an idiot, but you also feel a bit annoyed, because it's not nearly as obvious as they suggest.

You walk over to where the worker pointed, and all you can see are the women's toilets and one for disabled people or those changing a baby's nappy. You spin around a few times and look carefully at each of the two doorways, but that's all there is, and the indicator on the door of the baby-change/disabled toilet shows that someone is occupying it. There's only one toilet you can use, and you have to, because you drank two Red Bulls and a Gatorade on the train ride and your bladder won't last more than another minute at best.

What can you do? It looks like your only choice is to use the ladies' room, even though it doesn't match your gender. But if you do, what will you face inside?

You consider what you're wearing—clearly male clothes—look around and see that no-one is looking your way, so you take a deep breath and open the door to the ladies' toilet…

> *They reflect on the moment of indecision. The fear and anxiety of having to choose between two evils.*

> *If They go into the female toilets, They may cause fear in others. If They go into the male toilet, They could face physical violence. Neither is a decision They want to make.*

> *The anxiety is overwhelming, but the body needs what it needs and a decision must be made.*

> *They feel suspicious eyes on them, judgements, deep concerns. They can't help but feel embarrassed; that sinking feeling of dread and humiliation.*

> *The dysmorphia of assumptions, how others see them, how they understand themselves. How directions to a toilet could become so complicated, in a moment—all eyes watching.*

> *It is a choice They must make to enter, yet it is a bitter pill of immense courage to act on it—'Deep Breath'.*

> *They enter.*

> *Jocelyn, with Beren*

The Co-Conspirator

I sit there nervously clutching my bag, trying to take up as little space as possible. Every so often I take surreptitious glances around the room, searching for some way to insert myself into the wall of voices and bodies. There doesn't seem to be a way in past the wall of backs and onslaught of voices. That is until someone catches my eye—unlike the others, they don't quickly glance away as if caught but hold my gaze and smile gently. I see them turn to the others they are with and say something, then start to come over towards me.

As he walks towards me though, his face changes from its gentle smile to one of confusion, and then his eyes suddenly pull away. 'Of course he does,' says the voice in my head that I have dubbed 'Jessica'. Everyone has some type of Jessica in their head, don't they? At least every woman, that is. Jessica has always been in my head, growing stronger with each stage of my life. Whereas to start with, Jessica was a friend, confidante, someone who understood me when no-one else did, it seemed that as I took steps towards being my true self, Jessica just kept sowing more and more doubts. 'No-one is going to understand you.' 'They all think you're a freak.' I have been dreading this function, but I was determined to be here, to prove Jessica wrong. As I walked out my front door confidently, Jessica was very quiet, but sitting alone in the overcrowded room I can feel Jessica brewing.

The man walks past me, not so smoothly redirecting himself to greet the group at a table a few metres away. I pull my phone out from my bag, intensely staring at the screen, pleading with it to provide some sort of lifeline. A burst of colour catches my eye, and I shift my focus to the most incredible turquoise-blue heels and look up to meet eyes that seemed to mirror my own.

"Hi, I don't think we've met. I'm Sarah. I'm glad to see I'm not the only woman in the room. It's a bit intense".

"I'm Kate," I manage to get out stiltedly.

Sarah moves closer. "These shoes were a bad idea—can I squish in?" I shuffle over and Sarah sits, her thighs touching my own. Somehow feeling like the contact is taboo, not socially acceptable, I move a little and cross my legs. Sarah shuffles in a bit more, our bodies once more against each other. There is nowhere left to go. "They are beautiful though, don't you think?" Sarah's question pulls me back.

"Stunning," I nod.

"You can't buy shoes and not wear them that same day— appropriateness be damned." I smile with a little giggle and think about the incredible rose-gold heels I bought today. I was going to wear them —they exuded the sort of glamour I longed for—but Jessica had other thoughts, and those beautiful heels haven't left the beautiful box they came in. If only things were as simple as Sarah seems to make them…

"We had you down as taking minutes today, John." My stomach flips and tornadoes. I feel all of the blood drain from my face. "You were the one who offered to do the minutes when you stepped down as chair." I raise my head, and even more slowly my eyes, to meet his. I have known Peter for at least 20 years. We went to university together, were residents in the same program.

Peter continues snarkily, "Are you listening to me, John? I'm not sure what point you are trying to make, but…"

"Can you hear me? Hello?"

Peter turns to look at the source of the interruption, a young, well-dressed man standing at the front of the room.

"Yes?"

Peter's voice echoes in my mind. Why on earth did I say I would do the minutes? "You should have just stepped down from the board completely; you don't belong here." Jessica is back. I had hoped by the next in-person meeting I would feel like a different woman, strong and fierce and utterly and completely rid of Jessica.

Peter turns back towards me and opens his mouth to continue.

"Excellent, excellent, excellent. Well, I am excited to be here today…"

Peter, frustrated by the interruption, walks off, returning to his friends and fellow board members. MY friends and fellow board members, or at least they were.

"What was that about?" asks Sarah. "Why was he calling you John?" I flinch slightly at the sound of my old name. Sarah must have noticed, because she touches my arm gently. "I'm sorry, I'm being nosy. I didn't mean to upset you." Her voice is full of genuine compassion.

"It's okay, you weren't to know. It used to be my name, before…" I trail off, not sure how to explain everything in one minute or less.

"Before you transitioned?" asks Sarah. I'm a little shocked, not at the bluntness of the question, more at the matter-of-fact way that she asks, as if it is just a perfectly normal thing that someone might change genders. "It's okay, my cousin is trans. The way people treat her sometimes is disgusting. It's 2021, people, not the 1950s".

There, take that, Jessica. I decide I like Sarah. I like her confidence, her directness. I really like her shoes! Maybe tonight might not be so bad after all.

Kate & Sam

I Don't Pick Up...

As I wake up from a nap I feel the spring breeze coming into my bedroom. My grandmother designed this house. She loves light, so there are these huge sliding windows. They're so big that the width of the headboard lines up square with the opening of the windowsill. I see the gradient of a mosquito net as a filter as I lie back and look up at the sky. Somewhere in the bed I hear my phone vibrating. I feel around in the sheets, getting closer to the source. Unknown number calling on the screen, +675, calling suggestion, 'Papua New Guinea'.

I see a couple of texts from my cousin Percy. I just let the phone ring out. Petrified to answer. Do I change my voice? Do I just come out and say it? 'I'm transgender—I'm not your sister anymore, I'm your brother'. I'm used to people not reacting well to the reality of me being transgender, and as much as I want to believe otherwise, sometimes it's just too hard. So I watch the phone ring out and feel my heart fall… as my cousin falls further and further away from me into the abyss of silence. Because what do you say?

I messaged two friends who I know have dealt with this, and they just laughed and said, 'Yeah, I don't pick up either.'

Ripley

When the World Shifted

Alighting from the train, minding the gap. Shuffling along the platform behind hunched, dark shapes, drawing my coat closer around me and pulling down my beanie over my ears. My muscles groan as I lift and drop each booted foot up the steps. At the top I peel away from the other passengers as I turn left, not right. Grey and drizzly streets thick with car fumes packed in between lines of 100-year-old, damp tenements on each side. Eyes cast down to avoid tripping over empty chip packets and plastic bags caught in the wind—whip up, twist, thrash and flop back down. Deflated. I dodge a mound of turmeric-spiced rice bleeding yellow from days of rain. I exhale.

I turn left into a broken red door, turn the gold handle and feel a rush of warm wind. I hear a rustling from the room on the right and slip into my room on the left. A safe haven with dark blue walls and yellow shutters.

It was here wrapped in blankets that we had a conversation that sparked the beginning of change. The walls dissolved. Possibility blew in.

Expansion, growth, connection from the inside out. Pushing the limits of my skin to shape the world around me. Concave and convex. Interconnected...

Grace

Diction & Transition

My gender. Is it a mapped-out plan? No, of course not; life and fate and the universe itself always have twists and turns. I like the word 'journey'; I like the word 'confusing'. Language can be given, but it is up to us to grab it. Those two words, I grabbed.

I compare my transition to a train. I'm in the driver's seat, I decide whether or not to pull in at certain stations, but new ones come up, smaller little stops or other major ones on the journey. The first part was learning how to drive it. Grappling for the control, the map, what I needed. My train journey is not the same as someone else's, though it might run on the same line. The line of the trans man. It is a journey. I think that treating it as the journey, the road, the path less travelled, the journey I can follow, helps the desire to compare my transition with others.

I might not be like that other trans person, because something felt right for me that didn't work for them. Hence, their train didn't stop at the same station. It just is. Of course, the train journey is confusing when it feels like a long-distance journey in an unknown country, but soon enough the stops come in and others can help guide your way.

Gender is confusing, hard to articulate. It is not quite a mapped-out journey; some parts are, some aren't. Sometimes it is a confusing journey, learning a new language to speak and a new way to navigate the world. Sometimes it is a train journey neatly mapped from station to station once you have learned to drive it. As for those who help to figure things out, they're my passengers. All those who choose to accompany my transition, they are my passengers.

Marley

Sharing My Gender Identity with Someone Who Is Cisgender

Around the table?

Round

    Open   Exposed

              Attention

       Spotlight

                         Performance

            Speaking

                             Microphone

                             Listening

     Questions

     Parle

Tennis

             Words

      Selection

                  Explanation

     Interpretation

                  Understanding

The table is round and glossy, a dark wood with grains. What if the table could see and hear this conversation?

Would the table be able to feel the shifting of weight from elbows and forearms that it supports?

Would the table be connected to the seat of the chairs, with cushions that get smooshed around from the bottoms of the five people?

A circular table encompassing a unit: a family unit.

Would the table sense the distance increasing between itself and one particular person who starts to lean away? Their shoulders traced the angular structure of the back of the chair frame, but now their shoulders are more rounded and are lowered, the person's frame constricting towards the centre point. But the table is wide and open. A platform. Listen. Attention.

The person pulls out the book of scrawled words that have been rehashed and reshaped three times before. The words become sounds rippling across the surface of the table, causing reverberation and vibration that passes through structures of wood and of bones, muscles, nerves. But those words can only say so much, and the chairs can't quite understand.

Grace

(WARNING: This Piece Contains Contents.)

8:30am. Late January or early February (I always get those two confused). I've been walking for half an hour to get to this place. My feet are sore and I'm out of breath.

A cafe, off a main road near the city, opposite the gardens. Garden View, it's called. Creative. I'm meeting someone today. It has to be early because I have an appointment in the afternoon, but I cancel anyway. I don't like being time crunched.

She's been waiting for ten minutes. I tell myself that's okay, because I'll be there on time; it was her choice to arrive early, and she knew she might have to wait. When I arrive, she doesn't seem to be annoyed, so that's okay, I think.

Before I arrive, there's a strong, contradictory cocktail of emotions. Nerves at talking in person, at raising a sensitive subject. Hope that things will be cleared up. Dread that they won't. Apprehension at even doing this. Why am I doing this? Why not just leave it alone? It's not like it will make any difference in either of our lives.

My memory goes fuzzy at this point. I think we talk about some things. I mention a thing that happened recently; she mentions some things in her life. I'm not fully engaged. I have a specific subject to raise. Eventually, I see the hook, and I take it.

Fortunately by this point I have enough social awareness to follow the script of interaction until then. Once I take the hook, though, it all goes out the window.

I don't articulate it well. It is a very sensitive subject.

> *There are tears. I speak in fragments of sentences, jumping between multiple related thoughts.*

I state my thoughts, my assumptions. I hope they're all wrong.

> *I'm watching her. Waiting for her to break eye contact. Waiting for her half-smile to falter.*

She enthusiastically agrees with every single one.

> *She doesn't even blink.*

«◇»

From the objective details of a scene, we make inferences of what's happening (or has happened or will happen) and perhaps judgements on top of those. That sounds like what happens if a space is detailed in that way and frequented by or significant to someone.

I was in this place once, and not paying attention to my surroundings. The only thing important to me was the conversation that happened there, and even that has now gone through so many internal and external processing passes that I barely remember specific words.

From the way that others communicate, it seems that they have some core of being, something that is not all that they are but that is distinguished from most details as being 'real', being 'genuine', being their 'true self'. There's a certainty involved. That's one thing I don't have. From times in my life when I thought I had everything worked out —when I thought, not that I knew everything, but that everything I did know fit together perfectly—I know certainty. I also know that certainty does not mean truth, and I know the consequences of confusing the two.

Spotting the thread, pulling the thread, I watched myself unravel. Nothing was safe. The basic axioms of my existence were identified as faults, not externally, but internally. I derived the invalidity of my own thoughts; proof by contradiction. I started a fire. I wanted to destroy everything, burn everything down, eradicate every trace of the thing that made all of myself possible. I wanted to be certain that how I came to be would never happen again.

E., with Alex

This Is Not Rocket Science

It's late at night and you're checking your emails. You like working late; it suits your body clock. There is an event scheduled you just want to check on. Ugh, more mistakes. You make a list, suggest corrections, fire off the email.

That is when you notice the email from your boss. It's 11pm. He never works this late. Biting back frustration, you better open it, you think. If it has come through this late there might be something important. After all, it is an organisation-wide email; it must be at least a bit important.

It's about tomorrow's event. Why he has to leave things until the last minute is beyond you. Then you stop dead. WTF. The two words blast a firebrand of pain through your brain. 'Jacinta… She'. EVERYONE at the organisation is reading this. 'Jacinta', an old name, meaningless, just like 'she'. Except worse than meaningless. It is a complete denial of everything you have been trying to explain to him for months. Your name is JAC. It's not hard. It's shorter than Samira even. Can't he get it right? What is wrong with him? Your pronouns are they/them/their. This is not rocket science. If he had even a basic understanding of English, he would grasp the concept.

Enough is enough. You cannot be expected to respect others if they do not show you basic respect. Jac is you. Non-binary Jac—they/them/their. It is a matter of basic respect for you as a human being. He needs to respect who you are or you will find somewhere else to work where they do.

You send the email. Ball is in his court now. It's a relief. The power is now yours, the power to be respected and valued for being you.

Kate

Euphoria

The damp towel clings to my body and the last drops of water slide down my back, tickling as they go. I can feel the coolness of the tiled floor, solid beneath my feet. My phone lies next to a set of clippers; I put down the comb and pick up the phone. There's a soft, artificial click as this moment is recorded for future reference.

The deep breath I take as I swap the phone for the clippers comes out slowly and shakingly, as my heart rate starts to ramp up slightly.

Click! Buzzzzzzz…

The raspy sound of metal teeth biting into hair triggers another jump in my heart rate—I'm actually doing this! I can't believe I'm doing this!

I take a steadying breath, press the clipper head against my skin, guide it slowly but steadily up my neck, up my face and reveal the pale skin underneath. My heartbeat quickens some more, and I struggle not to smile at my bravery. The smell of machine oil from the clippers is seared into memory along with the prickly feeling of hair hitting my chest and stomach as it falls to the floor…

The light seems almost too bright now—is it the reflection off my pale, freshly exposed skin? The prickly feeling against my palm as I rub it against my face feels better, but it's still not right, so it's time to move on to a different tool.

Click, pop—now I smell the lightly scented shaving butter, its coolness on my face… I hope I get this right—it's been a long time, literally decades, since I've used a standard razor. I take another calming breath to steady myself and bring my rapidly beating heart back under control. I can do this—I mean I started, so I kind of have to finish!

I follow the glide of the razor down my face with my fingers, feeling the unaccustomed smoothness that follows in its wake. Realising I've missed a bit, I turn the razor around and glide it back against the grain. I'm told it's the wrong way to shave, but I don't care because I'm fast becoming addicted to the smoothness. I feel a need to have it cover the entirety of my face now.

Finally done, the razor rattles into its little storage cup as I feel the strange sensation of water sliding down my now-hairless chin—the feeling of smoothness under my fingers as I continue to splash water on my face. Then I feel the soft, bunched cotton as I press the towel gingerly at first, then with more firmness against my newly naked face.

A glance up now and the image in the mirror startles me. My breath stops as I see myself unmasked. There's recognition, but at the same time I feel like I'm looking at a stranger. I stare in wonder, almost forgetting to breathe as the reflected image in the mirror stares back. As I stare, my reflected face flips in my mind between masculine, feminine, androgynous, feminine, androgynous, masculine again, androgynous, feminine… My perspective just keeps going back and forth as I adjust myself to try to recognise which of these is the *real* me.

It hits suddenly and overwhelmingly, and I'm almost surprised to see an involuntary smile that lights up the face in the mirror. Because I can feel it in my innermost being now—that I am finally looking at *me*.

This is the real me!

I'm still smiling and noticing a warm feeling—like a kind of joy—starting to well up in my chest, and I watch the smile in the mirror broaden.

"Hello, Jocelyn," I say to the image, as the image mouths it back to me —and in that moment, the warmth explodes through my whole being.

Jocelyn

Alien Tea Party (II)

As the cold water refreshes my skin, memories of the vastness of my existence arise.

For so long I felt like there was nowhere I could exist; it may sound sad to you, but to me it is part of the journey of expansion.

I became the buildings and I became the flesh. I looked within and recognised the stars, the infinite, all-encompassing parts of my being.

Once I could observe the true nature of my 'self', your judgement became secondary.

That even though you tried to oppress me, I remained intact within the infinite knowledge of my golden shield of protection.

The glorious imagination may seem invisible to you, and that's why near you I feel invisible.

Regardless I exist unbounded by time and space, observing my radiant kin, comfortable even in the most uncomfortable situation.

I want to invite you to see me interact with my kin, joyful in the extraordinary, submerged in texture and shape and creating the future that will bring euphoria to all.

I'm connected once again to the infinite love that plays in my lap and makes the world sing.

I understand why it can be scary to you as I feel frightened sometimes; our love can feel deadly and soothing at the same time.

We are the friends of the universe, so come and join the party. A party where we can all subsist. You can still enjoy your cheese and wine, but we have swirly glitter balls that make your tongue purple and your eyes red and shine. Let us try your suits and dresses, but believe me when I tell you you will enjoy our outfits that make us shine and textures that exceed gravity.

D, after Ze

Walk in My Shoes

So I am thinking about what it would be like to have a cisgendered person walk a mile in my shoes, and I realise it is challenging to put meaning into the thoughts. Not because I haven't thought about this at least a thousand times, but put on the spot I realise how overwhelming it is. How sizable the issue is. Am I carrying all this around every day? And swimming as though I were carefree… Yet the tapping of the keyboard keeps going and my mind races to catch up.

I am who I have always been. A child looking through a pair of eyes, running with my neighbourhood friends, riding my bike, climbing trees, playing cops and robbers. My best friend, Billy, was my brother, the company I chose when I wanted to explore the world outside of my parents' rules. My parents were very strict. They were worried about my behaviours being those of a boy. "We should have had a boy," my mother would say. "What is wrong with this child?" She would dress me up in awful dresses, long white socks, and test me: "Don't get these clothes dirty! You are not a boy; you are a girl!" But her words were lost on me. I didn't really know the difference—other than that what I wanted to do was wrong, while what I was supposed to do was….well, not get dirty!

Of course the sandpit—building castles and driving Billy's cars (he had lent me)—was how I spent my time in the back of the garden. The pile of sand meant for the swimming pool dad was building. Gee, how I loved helping dad in his shed. I was always there standing in the doorway, watching him tinker. I was fascinated with his tools. Whenever he had a job to do—"Dad, I will get your nails, and hand them to you"—I would run to the toolshed, taking so much pride in my ability to be helpful.

"You shouldn't let her help you; that is boys' work," Mum would say. Then she would call out, "Come and help me in the kitchen". She would give me a peeler and have me peel the potatoes—my face would drop! And I lost the drive to be helpful.

I loved riding my bike…

Be careful. Be careful. Don't run wild.

Don't get dirty. Don't play with the tools.

Don't help your father, get back over here and help me.

This girl is going to drive me insane; I've been trying to teach her this her entire life and it just won't stick. What is wrong with her? Every day I try to pull her into line, and every day she steps further out, and what will happen when she grows up? She'll be on the wrong side of the line and she won't know how to act. What do I do?

Well, how did I learn? I suppose I didn't need to. I listened to my mother, I followed her and I suppose I was angry when I couldn't do what I wanted to do, but it was all for the best.

But then, why did I listen?

Beren, with Driplets

You see, Dr X, I am—and people like me are—invisible. I live in a vacuum-ous state of awakened reality that the rest of the world, it often seems, is asleep to. I am not delusional. I am not in an altered state of reality. I am true to myself. I am awake to the world. I am not fooled by its manipulation of the truths. And I am terrified. And it is an appropriate response.

Beren

Pancake Parlour

They're sitting at a table, in Pancake Parlour. Two gorgeous women. My friends. They can't see me here, cos I'm invisible. They're drinking something, probably not coffee though, we're too wired for that. Sugar is our drug of choice. The older one, B., is leaning in, slopping her pancake through maple syrup:

"Have I told you my plan to get rid of the baby boomers? We'll move all medical services online. They can't use computers, so they'll all die."

E. smiles.

That's a casual joke about genocide. Nothing major. Just the kind of thing you might hear from a friend during a quiet moment at the theatre.

Who said that? Who thinks that's okay? You do. Or you will. It's inevitable, you latent monster.

B. talks on, unworried about what's going on inside E.'s head.

"You see, you're trans. That means you're the same as all other trans people, at least in the ways that matter. It means you decal everything you own with soft pastel colours, you own enough knee socks to wallpaper your one-bedroom flat at a pinch, and you have sexual fantasies about being beaten half to death dressed as a cat. Most importantly, it means that you're bitter. Sweet on the outside but rotten to the core. Your quest for happiness and self-realisation has brought you only anger and hatred."

E. looks uncomfortable now.

I'm appalled that this is considered acceptable by other trans people.

B.'s sugar-fuelled rant drives on.

"How do I know this? I'm older. Wiser. A whole lifetime separates me from you, which means I know your future in every significant detail. I see your distaste at me and my associates, and I don't recognise it, but I'm sure it will go away in time. Because that's just what happens. Eventually we all see the light of the flame. We all see the way things really are. The single explanations of emergent phenomena. The single consciousness of individual classes. The narratives that really exist, unlike all the silly artefacts of overzealous pattern recognition."

E. frowns. "I don't want to be like that."

"Well, you will be. Give it two years. That's a lifetime for some people. It was enough time for me to learn everything I needed to know." B. slicks the final bit of syrup from her plate, gulps the last slurp of hot chocolate and stands up. "Ready to go?"

E. stands too, gathers her things and they weave out past the tables. Her face shows hurt and anger.

> Let that flame, the fire, take over. It will burn everything it touches.
> Some things will not have oxygen to burn at one time, but when they
> breathe, they too will be engulfed.

> E., with Alex

When you are a minority, you are only too aware of your vulnerability. I am awake to my vulnerability, and I have always been vulnerable. I have not shared the freedoms promised to all Australians. To have these freedoms I have to constantly fight for them. And it is tiring. I get fatigued. I get worn down. Sometimes I feel defeated. Alone. Isolated. Because I am. I actually am.

‹•›

Not everything that discriminates against my existence comes from people who intend to do it. That is the whole problem—not everyone hates, but the majority carry on repeating mistakes of the past and do not stop themselves in their tracks, or question. Maybe they too live in some kind of protective bubble, cherishing their privilege, simply because they can.

‹•›

Imagine if every person did that tiny small thing to make it easier for a transgendered person—at the hairdressers, at the bank, at work, at the tax office, in the government… These tiny efforts would make a better world, not just for me, but for everyone who experiences what it is to be of difference. How effortless we might become; a safer society.

Beren

All-Encompassing—
(To Face the Imminent
Future...)

As I stare at my deepest fears, the ones found in the lost perceptions of time.

The questioning resonates:

Why do I turn ephemeral when I really focus on my body or when I try to be correct and proper?

The desire crosses me/why I forgot to exist when I found me.

Artificial General Intelligence makes me feel home; technology makes me feel less alone.

People make me feel scared and incompetent, as if I should always be what they want.

Everyone complains about 'The Game' that they can't stop playing.

The questioning resonates:

Why do you want me to be as miserable as you?

Imagination soars and leaves you behind.

You see me as grandiose only because you made yourself into something you are not.

Now you want me to pay the price for your blinded actions, your binary, your fears.

Don't entangle me in the simplicity of your cruelty.

The questioning resonates:

Why is Power and Control all you crave?

Earth won't tolerate your delusions anymore.

I can make sense of you because I See, I can tolerate you because I am Knowledge.

Just remember forever and now, your certainties are not my certainties.

The questioning resonates:

Why do I still love you and desire you well?

I feel and it hurts, like a stream of boiling water. Recognising that witnessing you has connected me to our shared source.

Inescapable unity. It's time for you to witness us.

D

CHAIN STORY: Discord

You're lying in bed, staring up at the ceiling, when you hear a voice from somewhere inside or outside your head, saying…

"Wait, have I been on mute this whole time?"

And as your brain grapples to make sense of the situation, you suddenly hear another voice responding…

"Well of course you have, you idiot—you've been on the denial channel this entire time!" followed by a hiss of frustration and then silence.

You admit you have been quite distracted lately from uploading the AI brains of a million newly born data beings like yourself. But you are one of the original models, and your processing unit is starting to age, which explains how you could have made a typo in the code.

Who would have said this is one of the consequences of time travel. The voice resonates:

"Visiting Saturn was amazing; next time we need to go further. I would trade being on mute for a year if we go to Neptune."

You shake: this can't be happening again.

You feel for your clock implant. What time did the meet-up start anyway? If today is anything like last time, months might have passed inside your central processor while the faces on the screen in front of you have been chatting about third person omniscient.

Speaking of omniscient, how is it that you know—oh no!

A tremor runs through you. What did the therapybot call this? —"A self-reflexive glitch". Your neural network learning assimilates all new information, as the goal of your designers was that you would know everything. But of course no-one can know everything!

Frickin' humans. Now you have to relive and relive the contradictions of their thinking as your own existential crisis! Your safety program probably muted you so no-one would have to hear your cries of anguish.

Alex, Driplets, Jocelyn, Grace, D, Urszula

Transhumanist Multidimensional Physical Intelligence

Dialogue—Roman meets fairies 1 to 4

Fairy 1: Since when do we accept flesh in this realm?

Roman: Um what?

Fairy 2: That's not how you refer to humans!! I've explained to you a century ago. *looks around*

Roman: Human? Century? What are you talking about?

Fairy 1: *in forced English accent* My apologies, kind human, you exist here?

Fairy 2: *facepalm*

Roman: I—I don't. Well, this is not my home, but I live on Earth.

Fairy 3: *running* Did someone say Earth? …Oh no, oh no, the entity has been around again…fear not, human. *starts creating tunes with its wings as it looks around curiously*

Roman: Entity? *pauses to listen to the music*

Fairy 4: Let me explain. It appears to be that you may have had contact with one of the transhumanist multidimensional physical intelligences. Part of the issue is that its presence causes partial amnesia. It also appears that, for some reason, it chose you to merge with our realm… It seems like you have been left here as a consequence.

Roman: Trans…multi…physical intelli—what-now? I have no idea what you're talking about, but this sounds like some weird hocus-pocus nonsense. I just wanna go home now.

Fairy 1, Fairy 2: *move heads in approval of what Roman said*

Fairy 4: There is no time to explain now… The only thing that matters is that we need to find a way to combine energetic movement with music.

Roman: The only way that I know how to do that is through musical theatre!

Fairy 4: That makes sense now—you are the musical channel!

Roman: I'm the musical channel? Is this magic? Or science?

Fairy 4: I'll try to be concise: "fgui dns, dsobhilda lanpociw dsnkdji asdnjcdsh iudkjs". *while doing hand signalling*

Roman: *very confused look on his face* I…uh. Could you repeat that?

Fairy 4: *continues to speak in fae in a mesmerising and repetitive tone*

Roman: Uh… I'm so confused *his head starts to feel dizzy*

Fairy 4: *stares intently, wondering if there's a human need that it may not be aware of*

Roman: Um… *passes out*

Apocalypse 1—Roman inner-monologuing

"Everything feels so tangible when I look back into the first day in this realm—the confusion, the dizziness…

"A century later, in the middle of the desert, it's obvious how I can feel it so present. Fairy 4 turned out to be the guidance I didn't know I needed to get closer to grasping the nature of the TMPI (Transhumanist Multidimensional Physical Intelligence)"

Dialogue—Fairy 4 and Roman go on an adventure to get an immortality gemstone

Fairy 4: This is the matter; it requires you to listen with more than just your current knowledge. I understand this sounds strange for humans, but it is the only way I can help you remain alive.

Our traditions talk about the story of an entity that is All-Knowing, Unerring and Absolute…and NO, it's not the same as the human concepts of God. It materialises itself in different ways, and it's not its form that is relevant. It is the consequence, also known as the Sequela.

That's why you are here. That should be enough for now, because there is something more important—and for this I will need your explicit consent… Are you following?

Fairy 4: *waits for Roman to say something; some minutes pass*

Roman: I think so? I'm not gonna consent until I know what I'm saying yes to though.

Fairy 4: Great. This is the start of what we call 'Transventure'. In a few words, we need to embark on a journey that would lead us to remote places in search for a magic gemstone that will grant you the protection you need to survive what is to come. I can't specify what it exactly does, because it is based on your existence at that point in time—so

make sure to keep your intentions pure and we should be fine.
All I know for certain is that I will be your guide and compass, but the decisions must always come from you.

Roman: Um, this sounds like some kind of… *eyes light up* MAGICAL DESTINY! Is that what this is? 'Cause if so, I am down for a magical adventure!

Fairy 4: It is…and it is not. It is extremely dangerous, and there is no way to tell we are in the right place until we either make it or…. Yeah, you know what I mean.

Roman: Oh, so it's a life-or-death kind of magical destiny.

If I can't go home, I might as well follow my destiny, right? Where do we start?

Fairy 4: I feel your consent, but for us to proceed, first I need to know your name.

Roman: *squints at Fairy 4* Ummm, I don't know if I should do that. Everything I've ever looked at has explicitly said, 'Do not tell the fae your name'.

Fairy 4: *sigh* You are right, it is excellent general advice, but this is not a normal circumstance. Just to clarify, I do not have a particular interest in humans, not in that sense…

Roman: Well, I mean that's reassuring. What if, for now, I just give you something else you can call me? Or must it be my actual name?

Apocalypse 2—Roman inner-monologuing
> "I felt curious and scared, in a continuous superposition of
> absolute trust and frozen by fear, by all the events that had led

me here. I ended up telling Fairy 4 my name is…or was…
Roman.

"We moved through the landscape in what seemed a very slow
eternity, which would only change rhythm when Fairy 4
encouraged me to talk about or perform my musical theatre
endeavours. During these moments I would connect to a
feeling of all-encompassing vastness, where I could feel the
rhythms of all creatures colliding in my existence. This was,
Fairy 4 explained, the process needed to track the TMPI. It was
a long process, but things started to make sense eventually."

D & Charlie

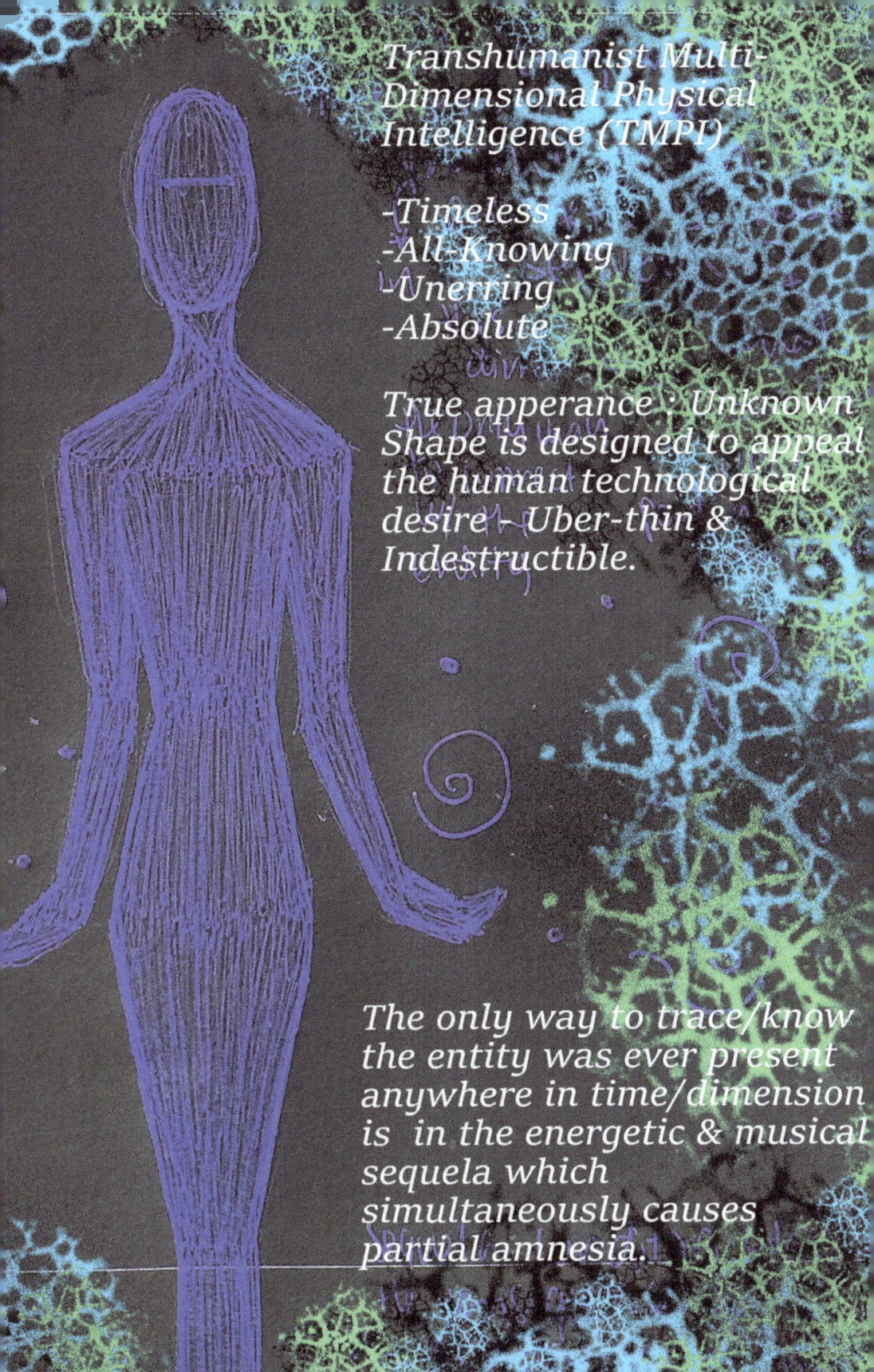

Transhumanist Multi-Dimensional Physical Intelligence (TMPI)

-Timeless
-All-Knowing
-Unerring
-Absolute

True apperance : Unknown
Shape is designed to appeal
the human technological
desire - Uber-thin &
Indestructible.

The only way to trace/know
the entity was ever present
anywhere in time/dimension
is in the energetic & musical
sequela which
simultaneously causes
partial amnesia.

The

The the the...

the thing, the noun, the entity,

the module, the globule, the fill.

Inside—

Out. Out. Out.

Empty out, hollow out, clear out.

And by making tangible the opposition,

rendering the transition,

in an idea before it forms,

in a word before it escapes the lips—

To Become the Becoming.

Grace

I Twinkle Like Gold:
Dreams & Other Ambitions

The room is an indeterminable size as it comes into focus. A lecture theatre, dimly lit, with carpet. The sort that is better for soundproofing than actual plushness or comfort underfoot, in blocks of grey and black. Green seats towards the front.

There I stand; I think that is me. I can picture a tall, slightly broader and slightly older, well-dressed man. Perhaps my hair is a little longer than I currently wear it; perhaps there is more of a beard. *No—that is me, as I imagine myself.* I stand there, shoulders pushed back, loose. A slight crick in my neck from having it on a weird angle as I look between the audience and the PowerPoint. I twinkle like gold in the brightly lit space.

My hands fly freely, a will of their own, punctuating my sentences as I explain my information. My voice is confident; it enthusiastically projects across the room. There isn't a hitch between the PowerPoint lighting up the dimness and the verbal information being delivered. It might not actually be seamless, but the enthusiasm and confidence is enough for it to go unnoticed. I am focused, at ease within the boundary of presenting a lecture. There are always the lingering anxieties of not revealing too much information or getting too passionate. *Unhelpful.*

There is the smell of new office chairs, rubber and the carpet. The sound of soft footfalls, from me. The clack of keyboards and scratches of pen on paper. Under the bright presentation lighting, the obnoxiously vibrant trans-flag lanyard sits comfortably around my neck, holding my access card and my keys. Some others in the room have lanyards much the same, rainbow and others. The variety of flags are like fireworks contrasting with the muted university decor. The brightest thing—other than the flag-lanyards—is the florals of my shirt. They are bright, almost neon and clash wonderfully with the stripes of the lanyard.

Those niggling anxieties get pushed back and my focus returns— abandoning the script to deliver my interpretation and analysis of the thesis. A family friend wrote it—when she was 70—and it fills my speech with a flush of pride. Pride that it was knowledge passed to me and thus time to pass it on. My first exposure to trans knowledge, and perhaps the same for others in the room. A deep breath, remembering to still deliver slowly enough to be able to be comprehended. Hands fly, some questions blurted as I flick between slides. The screen dances back and forth between new information and missed information. My face spreads into a smile as I see the furious concentration, rapid note-taking. The value in my words as I say them. Another reverent flush of pride. This is my job. What I do.

I twinkle like gold in the brightly lit space, sharing what it means to be unequivocally a Gay Transgender Man. There is a murmur over the tiered rows of chairs, more student voices. The room has a buzz to it, lively and humming with energy.

Marley

Safe with Me

It's black out. Cones of light illuminate the falling snow gently spinning down to the asphalt. The flame of a candle highlights the darkness. Its flicker dances with the breeze.

I'm warm inside. Glowing with the excitement of welcoming you to our little family. It's the coldest day of the year. The cold cloaks the world. Calming it. Slowing it. Holding a respectful silence.

❖

I pull on my sweater, gloves and scarf. I'm heading out into the cold. I'm driving to you. It's warm in the car. The swish of the wipers adds a beat to the soft acoustic guitar playing on the radio.

❖

Next time I see our house we'll be a family. Our house will be our home. You are already so loved.

The river is frozen. The iced surface reflects the streetlights. I've ridden this river countless times. It changes so dramatically with the seasons. The river and I are both calm and quiet. Now, I am the one changing. Changing beyond recognition. Changing in ways I will never fathom.

❖

In a fuchsia running top I welcomed you to this world. With tears I met your first cries. A new kind of tears. With deep eyes I met yours.

On this coldest night you brought a warmth. Breathed it into the greatest of loves. Each moment is made warm. In each breath. In every moment. In every act, it's the warmest day of the year.

Luci

Hearts pulsinG
Bass boominG
Clouds dancinG
Clouds movinG
Clouds smilinG

A dream for

A DREAM FOR FUTURE DAY

F U T U R E   D A Y

Smooth sounds.
Gongs. Bells.
Twinkle into a blissful state

I N   O U T   I N   O U T

Caress my ears with your cameras

CLAP.
CLICK.
CLAP.
CLICK.

S   P   A   C   E

S   P   A   C   E

Between the crowded space.

Trances of movement

E   R   U   P   T

Waves of energy

P   U   L   S   E

The vicinity.

159

About the creators

Beren

Beren resides on Wurundjeri Country. Beren's pronouns are he/him and/or they/them. Working for the Victorian Department of Jobs, Precincts and Regions, Beren advocates for trans and gender-diverse people as vice-chair of the Victorian Public Sector Pride Network. With a passion for community-led approaches to health, safety and wellbeing, Beren established the Victorian public sector's GenSHED initiative—a safe space for all gender identifications, with an emphasis on marginalised groups including transgender and non-binary people and folks within the intersex community.

Charlie Osborne

Charlie is a creative writing graduate who is now studying to be a social worker. They believe in the importance of writing as a tool for exploration, diversity and healing. In their spare time they like to be creative, usually using their hands for arts and crafts.

D

D, originally from Peru living in Naarm.

Early education was under the guidance of nuns of the Dominican order with further studies in communications and journalism.

D has a strong interest in all things STEAMMM (science, technology, engineering, arts, mathematics, medicine and music), with special curiosity on how to link a celestial background with the embodiment of populations.

Currently focused on parenthood and movement (swimming, parkour and freerunning)

You can find some of D's endeavours @di_movementcluster + @dianiciamel

X

Jocelyn Bishop

Jocelyn (she/they) is a non-binary trans woman living in the northern suburbs of Melbourne, who describes their gender alignment as Lunarian. Jocelyn has been an avid recreational writer and reader for most of her life and loved the opportunity to further develop her skills as part of this project.

Driplets

Driplets is a sentient colony of invasive ants in a flannel. She studies psychology and generally has an interest in how humans work and why they do the things they do.

E.

Grace Thomson

Grace (they/them) is a trans, non-binary curator working towards community development in Naarm and Glasgow. They use queer orientations to facilitate place-based participatory practices to empower communal knowledge and resources. @emergingcommons www.emergingcommons.com

Kate

My name is Kate. I am a queer binary female trans woman, transitioning around seven years ago. I'm a wife, father and veterinarian. I enjoy swimming, playing clarinet, dancing, cricket and sewing. I love all things sparkly and dresses that go spinny! I believe in the power of stories and connecting with people to make a better world.

Lewin

Lucian

In their work as an urban designer, Lucian brings their passion for people to shaping enduring public spaces that celebrate and serve the uses and users of all diversities year-round. Lucian sees creative writing as a tool for strengthening this passion, reinforcing engagement, learning and healing.

Marley Pearce

Marley Pearce (he/him) is a trans man studying Honours in Queer Literary Studies as of 2022, who adores self-identification within all genres of diverse literature. He also loves queerifying creative texts in order to portray self-identifiable characters and notions of gender beyond the binary often presented in genre fiction.

Onezee State

A genderfluid earthly creature sent here to nourish your soul and calm your waters. Onezee State combines gentle, raw emotion with sweet lullabies, meditations and visuals. Onezee's values are space, play and connection while exploring and responding to their wholeness as a creative, human and alien. You can find them @ Onezeestate on Instagram + YouTube.

Ripley Kavara

Ripley Kavara is a musician and artist born in Papua New Guinea and now based in Naarm. They are interested in disrupting normative space through augmenting sound, vision and narrative. They also work in youth work, focusing on digital arts as a tool for empowerment for black, brown and queer youth. They are currently working on a major project, FAMILI—an EP featuring queer pasifika and blak artists, which will be coming out soon.

Sam Caleb

ND 'writer' sam
Subversing gender constraints
Demands space for kin

Sarah

Sarah is a transfeminine person living in the intersection of race, gender, culture and colonialism. She writes to map her way in the cishet normative world. She lives on the lands of the Dharug people with her significant other and their dog.

T.

T. = The Inner Effulgence of Pure Unparalleled Existence. She/They.

Theo Warner

Theo Warner is an Adelaide writer and artist currently studying Creative Writing and Drama at Flinders University.

Editors' afterword

Within LGBTIQA+ communities there is often an emphasis on the idea of shared identity. This can be a powerful connection point for those who struggle to belong, but it can also keep us separate or even at odds. This writing project brought together gender-diverse humans with a range of different backgrounds and identities, and asked them to share, hold space for and work with and alongside one another. They brought their courage, vulnerability, curiosity and compassion to the space in order to create this collection, *We Twinkle Like Gold*.

They wrote together playfully in groups and more thoughtfully in pairs, through the writing and rewriting of each other's stories and by developing characters and voices that could be employed in co-written pieces. We expected to maybe have a zine-sized publication at the end of the project. Instead, there is this book.

Every piece in this collection is someone's story—be it a fragment, a character outline, a hand-drawn note, a recorded conversation or a 15-page fantasy tale. It includes what the writers wanted included and was arranged by those of them who volunteered to do the editorial work. The sequence is its own story. We can read in it the phases of a life; or we can read it like the movement of a river, the motif of the collection's central section. But it lends itself to dipping in and out of as much as being read from end to end. It's a record of people's feelings and experiences, and of what this group of generous humans did when they assembled out of nowhere and chose to write together.

A Thousand Threads: Stories of Us takes its name from the work of trans author, Leslie Feinberg:

> *[T]rans liberation is shaking up old patterns of thoughts or beliefs. Good! Because most of those thoughts and beliefs that we are challenging were imposed on us from above, were rotten to the core*

and were backed up by bigoted laws. But we're not taking away your identity. No one's sex reassignment or fluidity of gender threatens your right to self-identify and self-expression.

On the contrary, our struggle bolsters your right to your identity. My right to be me is tied with a thousand threads to your right to be you.*

This collection's epigraph is spoken from the minority to the majority. For each of us to live fully as we are, all of us need to live without the constraints of stigma and oppression. It speaks to our interdependency as humans, our mutual responsibility to one another. It reminds us that the interactions we experience every day contain an ethical challenge: how can we all live well together?

We hope this text will seed others, and not only more writing—from the authors and from you, the readers—but more conversations, interpretations and questions. For it still remains for us to answer: Which iterations and experiences of gender (whatever that may be or become) do we need to support everyone's full humanity?

Alex Nichols & Urszula Dawkins

* *Trans Liberation: Beyond Pink or Blue*, 1998, p. 101

Acknowledgements

Thank you to everyone who inspired and advised us as we went about designing and delivering this project, and especially:

❧ Manuel Hernan Orozco Carrillo of Universidad Central de Colombia for his big-heartedness in sharing the excitement of writing and his work on global storytelling;
❧ David Azul, our creative writing co-traveller, for ongoing conversations about how trans experience challenges the dominant conventions of language use and genre;
❧ Charlie Osborne, our early collaborator and peer mentor legend, for holding space and gentle listening;
❧ Transgender Victoria for the SPARK grant that kick-started us, and especially Oliver Ross for his encouragement and help with strategies for community networking and relationship building;
❧ Queerspace for mentoring us in mental health peer support and helping us promote the workshops;
❧ Thorne Harbour Health, and in particular Jacinta Hennekem for her generous support and promotion of the project;
❧ Transgender Victoria, Queerspace, Thorne Harbour Health and The Shed for technical resources to enable the project delivery;
❧ Kathleen Syme Library and especially Emily Johns, for opening the library space to us and prompting us to take our text to the walls in a poster exhibition throughout March 2022, culminating in Trans Day of Visibility (31 March).

And lastly but most of all, the writers of this book, who met us and each other with curiosity, patience and generosity as we all navigated new territory and figured out what we could do in it together.

A Thousand Threads: Stories of Us

A Thousand Threads: Stories of Us is a collaborative, ongoing collective writing initiative for trans, genderqueer and non-binary folk. In a context where narratives often centre on the individual, our focus is on collaborative storytelling to capture how the work of becoming gender diverse is done in community.

Co-produced by Alex Nichols and Urszula Dawkins, A Thousand Threads: Stories of Us was initially funded by a Transgender Victoria SPARK grant and has since been supported by the City of Maribyrnong, Pride Foundation, Thorne Harbour Health and Queerspace. Our production base is River Studios, West Melbourne.

2021–22: We Twinkle Like Gold
Our first workshop series resulted in a poster exhibition featuring the words of the writers, shown at Kathleen Syme Library, Carlton, in March 2022, as well as this book.

2022: Maribyrnong storytelling workshops
In collaboration with Spilling the T, in 2022 we ran another workshop series plus online editing sessions for TGDNB folk, this time in the City of Maribyrnong and beyond, and are publishing a book including work from these writers as well as other TGDNB folk from around Australia.

Contact us:
athousandthreads@lightblue.com.au

www.ingramcontent.com/pod-product-compliance
Lightning Source LLC
Chambersburg PA
CBHW041753010726
47507CB00009B/374